PETER TOPSIDE

LOVE AND PIECES

A SUPERNATURAL HORROR STORY

Love and Pieces

Copyright © 2023 Peter Topside

Published by Meadowsville Quill, LLC

Paperback ISBN: 979-8-9886116-0-8
Hardcover ISBN: 979-8-9886116-1-5
eISBN: 979-8-9886116-2-2

Cover and Interior Design: GKS Creative
Project Management: The Cadence Group
Developmental Editing: Monti Shalosky
Copyediting and Proofreading: Kim Bookless

This is a work of fiction that contains graphic violence, strong language, and psychologically distressing elements.

All Rights Reserved. No part of this book may be reproduced or transmitted in any form or by any means, electronic or mechanical, including photocopying, recording, or by any information retrieval or storage system, without the prior written consent of the publisher.

I can't believe I've written four books! It's only appropriate that I dedicate this to my wife and daughter, to The Cadence Group, and to Monti Shalosky. Without all their care and support, my books would never have come to fruition.

Author's Note

The first chapter of *Love and Pieces* takes place during the final portion of one of my previous books, in *Preternatural Reckoning*. I divulge enough information to bring the reader up to date on what is necessary, but *Love and Pieces* does not have any other connection to my prior trilogy. It is its own unique story, despite taking place in the same world that my other books do. Enjoy!

Prologue

A Tuesday morning in the biggest little town in America, Meadowsville, showed a community in disarray. The once busy and profitable area had suffered a tremendous downturn in the previous few weeks. After many scandalous years dealing with vampires, political corruption, and a divided town, the present day yielded no difference to the past. All of its residents went about their daily business, unsure whether their lives were at jeopardy from the villainous creature Blackheart. This vampire had held the town in its grasp for many years, with no end in sight, ruthlessly killing its citizens like meaningless cattle.

Chapter 1

Camille Pierce sat in a call center in Meadowsville's business district. She wore a light gray short-sleeve polo that read *Organic You!* Her lean frame slouched forward, her elbows rested on the padded wrist support, and her brown eyes resisted the urge to close. As she scanned the assigned call list of unsuspecting individuals, dread over what would happen after the line started ringing sank in. Her nicely manicured fingernails gently pressed each key on the phone as it dialed out. She admired her nails and how well they turned out, despite being done with dollar store products. Times were tough in Meadowsville over the last year. Company profits were down and costs were up, so even being able to hold this job down was a blessing. Things used to be so different here, up until the supposed return of the Blackheart phenomena.

The line rang, and the persistent thought of how selling weight loss plans became a career filled her mind. She was stuck in a cubicle with no prospects of a boyfriend, advancement in the company, or ambition of doing more with life. The ceiling vent blew cold air across the back of her neck, making her dark brown ponytail sway. The walls of the cubicle were the same color as her shirt.

If I sit completely still, could I just blend in? No one would see me. Then I really could take that nap. Maybe something to eat first, because I haven't had anything since yesterday. When it comes down to rent or food, rent takes the lead.

Mr. Anderson walked by in his usual disheveled suit. It was a very unflattering chocolate brown that made him look like he got it out of a low-end thrift store or even possibly out of a dead relative's closet. He had forgotten to tuck in the back of his shirt, and as he walked, the unrestrained fabric danced along to his feet scuffling across the floor. His somewhat curly hair hung across his forehead, always leaving his peers curious whether it was greasy or just had too much product in it. And he always appeared to be sweating. Not a dripping sweat but a general glistening of sorts. Camille smiled, wondering why someone as large as Anderson could be in a managerial position at a weight loss product company. It just seemed ironic.

He's probably some bigwig's idiot relative that he owed a favor to somehow. Must be nice to have good ole-fashioned nepotism working in your favor. Lord almighty, I'm so judgmental.

He always ogled the women in the office, which Camille never got used to. And he would peer at her specifically. Not that she felt like she was anything special, but his gaze left her unsettled every single time. It wasn't just a look of curiosity or of someone with awkward social skills. Like that of a predator observing its next meal. Hungry, craving eyes.

I wish I could hide under my desk and not be seen by anybody. I hate how he watches me.

Anderson pretended to fix the papers that he carried in under his left arm but did so just to leer back at Camille. His usual breathlessness was more noticeable today, and his mouth opened slightly as he looked at her.

Oh God, I want to jump out of my skin.

A cold shiver went through her spine, and she straightened up, pushing through the feelings.

"Hello," a burly-sounding man answered on the other line.

I hope they don't yell. I can't stand when they yell.

"Morning! My name is Camille, and I'm calling from Organic You. Is this Charles? How are you today, sir?" she asked with a pronounced perkiness to her voice.

"Um, I'm well. What is this?"

"Organic You! You had answered a consumer survey last month and stated that you may be interested in trying some of our products."

"I don't remember doing a survey," Charles responded sternly.

This could go either way.

"I believe it was from PennyForYourThoughts.com."

There was a long pause and heavy breathing into the line.

Camille wondered whether that was what Mr. Anderson sounded like close-up. She shivered again and resisted the urge to gag.

"Oh, I remember now," the man replied, expressing less resistance.

"Great! So I wanted to take this opportunity to tell you about some of our exciting weight loss products . . ."

"What is it, like a pill or powder?" he interrupted.

"We actually have both forms for most of our supplements. And all of our products are made with only organic ingredients to ensure you're getting nothing but the best in your body. Creating a truly organic you! Because you deserve to feel your best. And we can get you there."

The line went quiet, but the heavy breathing persisted. "I'm actually a little busy right now. Can we do this some other time?"

"Yes, absolutely. I know how crazy Tuesdays can get. What is a good time and day that I can reach out to you again?"

The phone clicked after being hung up, and Camille leaned back in her chair, taking a deep breath.

I prefer when they just hang up. The yelling drives me batty.

She selected "Not interested" on her computer screen next to Charles Spencer's name. A quiet alarm went off on her cell phone, indicating that her fifteen-minute coffee break had arrived.

I hope someone left something in fridge from yesterday. I'm starving.

Camille got up and stretched her lower back briefly before heading to the break room. For such a plain-looking office environment, the break room was rather nice. She passed by the endless rows of cubicles, hearing each of her colleagues reciting the same script she had repeated tens of thousands of times. It was always amusing to see the energy of the new hires versus the lacking enthusiasm of the more seasoned staffers. The newbies felt they were all special and could climb that corporate ladder rung by rung but had no idea their pursuit was no different than being a hamster on an exercise wheel. They could work themselves to death and there would never be a promotion, significant pay raise, or anything to give them the proper credit for their efforts. Most of them would burn out within the year and leave the company, while a select few would wind down and go into a work mode that she referred to as cruise control. That was where she found herself nowadays.

This company should do before and after shots of everyone hired each year in a nice demotivational Christmas card. She laughed at the thought.

She reached the community coffeepots and poured a cup of decaffeinated coffee. The odor of burned overflow struck her sinuses hard, and she winced a bit. She looked down at a newspaper sitting on the one table, with a front-page article from the *Meadowsville Quill* reading "Blackheart Is a Fraud? Is Meadowsville's Savior a Devil in Disguise?"

She attempted to pick it up and read further about the long-lived legend of Blackheart in what had been her town for several years now, but the paper stuck to the table. The destruction and death that Blackheart had already caused and the fact that the monster was still running around out there always amazed her. But she never was directly impacted by any of the tragedies or issues, so it was a nonfactor for her. She wanted to care more, but she just couldn't. Her mind was always elsewhere.

This town is ridiculous. I need to get out of her as soon as I can. What I wouldn't give for a massive raise so I could save up enough to leave. Then again, God only knows what other towns are dealing with if we have this kinda stuff here.

Footsteps entered the room behind her, and her colleague Annette walked in. Annette was one of those older ladies who worked just to give herself something to do and had a delightful don't-give-a-shit-and-won't-take-no-shit-from-anyone kind of attitude. Her husband had passed away several years ago, and aside from playing with her half dozen grandchildren on the weekends, bickering with people about weight loss products was a good form of entertainment for her.

She coughed and poured a cup of coffee for herself, looking at the paper and then Camille. "It's fuckin' amazing that we can put a man on the moon and have smartphones but can't stop this thing from destroying the town. Fuckin' crazy, right?"

Camille smiled and laughed. She liked Annette a lot. They always had good interactions, and she was one of the handful of coworkers who weren't interested in stepping on each other's backs in order to progress in the company. Annette just did her job, didn't exude a bit of anxiety or stress, and went home. Simple and straightforward. Camille hoped to be just like that one day. Stable and settled.

Damn, that's a nice thought. Well, in a different job, that is.

"You're right. I've only been in the town for a few years, but I've never seen anything like this in my life. Like a real-life devil running around in broad daylight," Camille responded.

Camille thought back to her upbringing in Festiville, which was a smaller, simpler town than Meadowsville. Or as the locals would joke, it was just one of the many *villes* in the area. But every town had its urban legends and monster sightings. However, Blackheart was like nothing else known to man. The stories she had read online and heard being passed around the office made her thankful she'd never been affected by that entire situation. Blackheart was akin to some biblical plague.

Annette sat down at the table, letting her myriad of bracelets jingle against each other. "And the worst part is you don't know who to believe because of all those assholes running this place." She rested against the table and slurped her coffee a bit, not taking her eyes off Camille. "All crooked with an agenda just to suit themselves. And it's poor schmucks like you and me just trying to go to work, pay our bills, and not get involved." Annette motioned to the seat across from her. "Sit down, honey. You're making me nervous. An old lady like me can't get nervous, or I'll drop dead and you'll feel guilty forever."

Camille sat down and watched the clock to be sure she was back at her desk at the fifteen-minute mark. Mr. Anderson, while very rotund, could move surprisingly fast when he needed to and especially loved catching the female staff being tardy. He would wave his red pen and taunt each of them, saying things like "I could warn you this time. But that wouldn't teach you anything. I'm writing this up and putting it your file."

Camille curled her lip a bit, thinking of the few times he had done that to her. And it was never done in a professional way, behind a closed door in a meeting room or office. He did it publicly to embarrass and humiliate, which he took pleasure in.

"So you're such a pretty young thing. Any guy would be lucky to be with you. Give me a cheap thrill and tell me about your love life," Annette beseeched in her raspy voice, grinning.

Camille pursed her lips and thought momentarily before responding. "Not much going on there, Miss Annette. I've been covering a lot of extra shifts for a while so I can save up enough to move. This town is not where I want to stay long-term."

"I get it. Too much bullshit here. Find some place simple and quiet. Find a good man, pop some kiddies out, and work someplace where they appreciate ya. Or at least pay ya enough to spit on you but keep you coming back for more. Not my style. Too kinky, if you catch my drift, girlie." She winked at Camille.

Camille smiled at the lovely thought of all that and hoped to make it a reality at some point. Her stomach growled and Annette laughed.

"Better get something in there. Just raid the fridge and steal a lunch bag with one of the new kid's names on it. They're too shy and nervous to accuse anyone of taking their food."

Suddenly, a series of loud, ground-shaking crashes shook the entire building. Annette and Camille braced themselves, coming out of their conversation. When the rumbling stopped, they cautiously stood up and looked out the nearest window.

LOVE AND PIECES

Their view of the downtown area showed buildings collapsing one after the other. Explosions and cars skidding off the roads, trying desperately to avoid falling debris. Meadowsville was being destroyed right in front of their eyes. But unlike past instances with Blackheart, this looked like it had the ability to finally do the ultimate job.

A loud alarm went off from every smartphone in the office, silencing the screams from the people in the office. Everyone jumped and grabbed at their phones to see the following message—

> Meadowsville is under attack.
>
> Go inside immediately and stay inside your house or building.
>
> Bring pets indoors only if you can do so quickly.
>
> Close all windows and doors.
>
> Turn off air conditioners and heating system blowers.
>
> Close fireplace dampers.
>
> Gather radios, flashlights, food, water, and medicines.
>
> Call 911 only if you have a true emergency.
>
> You will be advised when this dangerous situation has passed and it is safe to go outside and resume normal activities. Please be patient with emergency services, and further information will be relayed as it becomes available.

The building shook again. Several large windows broke and sent shards of glass down to the people on the street below, eliciting more screams of terror. Annette lost her footing and stumbled backward into the wall. Camille ran forward and checked to see she was okay.

"Let's get out of here before the building gives out," Camille said, helping Annette to her feet and noticing a small wound on the back of her head.

It's going to be okay, Annette. Just stay with me.

Annette was not able to walk well and seemed very disoriented. They made their way to the cubicle area, aiming for the stairs, but hordes of their colleagues shoved past each other, all going in that same direction.

Another loud crash occurred, but this one was different. This was from directly underneath them. The tile floors began to separate and crack, opening up to show the level below them. Camille saw Blackheart for the first time. And it was utterly terrifying. A true, real-life monster.

He was holding what looked to be a corpse, using it as a battering ram, crushing anything in their path. The dragon-like creature snarled and couldn't care less about anything going on around it. It was focused on inflicting the maximum amount of pain possible on its former abuser, John Smith. They plowed down through several more levels until Camille was able to see down to the lobby from the sixth floor. There were more eruptions, momentarily interrupting the screaming and panic that had overtaken the building.

What are we going to do?

More of the floor fell through, and the building started to shift, losing more of its stability. Annette stopped Camille as they made their way away from the now collapsing emergency stairway. Dozens of people were crushed and trapped.

There's no way out!

"Don't be stupid. Go save yourself. I'm done for." Annette pushed Camille off shortly before she fell backward into the gaping hole behind them.

"Annette!" Camille screamed but knew it was futile. Her friend was dead. And a cloud of dust flew up and greeted her face, blinding her and making her cough profusely.

She ran to the sink to wash her face and noticed the sudden silence. The calm before the storm. Then the building began to fall. Camille grabbed onto anything around her, settling on the pipes under the sink.

Oh God. I'm not going to make it. I'm going to die!

Like she was living in a nightmare, she held on with superhuman strength, watching the walls crumble, the ceiling fall, and the floor give out from beneath her. She screamed again, continuing to hold as the pipes bent and twisted. Her legs were crushed under the debris, and pure fear enveloped her as she lost consciousness, falling into oblivion. Meadowsville was totally destroyed, and Camille was, just as in her job setting, another faceless victim. Her hopes and dreams would never come to fruition. In her final moment, as she plunged down, she questioned which would be worse—to die or be alive in a hopeless situation.

***

Tens of thousands of its citizens lay dead, scattered across the once tranquil terrain. A cloud of smoke blurred the visibility of nearly every part of the town. The occasional cry for help could be heard, but they were far and few. Not even emergency responders were able to do anything at the time.

Blackheart had accomplished the first part of his quest. He flew over the town, smirking and admiring his handiwork. His newly manifested physical form resembled a hideous flying demon. The town that hurt him so badly and allowed so many atrocities to occur was no more. Now he could move on to his ultimate war with God.

He laughed, watching the few survivors try to get out from under debris. He could help them without issue but didn't care. They all deserved to suffer as much as he did. He hovered gracefully over some of the survivors and asked them to willingly pledge their allegiance to him. Some refused, while others couldn't respond in time, so he simply left them to die.

Chapter 2

I'm alive...

Camille opened one eye and saw the reddish sky through the mountain of debris around her, but she was trapped. Major injuries had been sustained over her entire body. Her legs were broken, she was possibly missing her left eye, and she could barely move. The debris was too heavy. She pushed as hard as she could, but nothing budged.

How long was I out? Hours? Days?

"Help me! Someone please help me!" she screamed with all her might, but there was just silence.

She tried again to push some of the debris and was able to free her legs. They scraped and split open under the pressure of the cement from the building, but she had no feeling in them, so it didn't affect her. They just felt like lead weights hanging off her hips.

"Help!"

But again, there was no response.

She began pushing at the opening, hoping to create a bigger airhole, but was only able to get her face out. The smell and appearance of the town resembled a warzone.

"Help!"

At first, there was no response, but then suddenly, when Camille began to give up hope, she heard something. A large shadow was cast over her from the sky above.

"Do you believe in me as your true savior?" the deep, bellowing voice asked her.

Blackheart. He was truly real, and this was all actually happening. Any doubts about the authenticity of his presence and abilities were now answered. But she was confused as to what he was asking her.

"Do you believe in me as your true savior?" he repeated as the few rays of sunshine illuminated his leathery bluish skin, the light somehow able to penetrate the dust and smoke encasing everything.

What is he talking about? What's happening?

While she wasn't an atheist or an avid churchgoer, she knew this monster was not something she wanted to believe was a deity of some sort. Agreeing with an abomination like this could not result in anything positive.

"No," she spit out. "No, I don't."

Blackheart sneered and landed on the ground, mustering up even more dust around his body. He offered his gnarled, clawed hand to Camille, as if to help. As she reached for it, he purposely scraped her palm and pulled back, knocking more debris over her small opening. He then slowly rose off the ground and left her.

Camille lost her grip, fell face-first into the ground, and began crying.

He just left me here! What am I gonna do? I would've been better off dead.

She pushed up to a seated position and leaned against the dome of wreckage around her. Broken glass and cement, singed building materials, and the occasional bloodied street sign all painted a vivid picture of the disaster that had been dealt to Meadowsville that day.

She then noticed Mr. Anderson was sitting across from her. His body was contorted and bloodied, with only half his face intact. The rest of his body was missing skin and most of his clothes. His eyes were both open and watched her, giving her that lecherous, uncomfortable stare she had worked so hard to ignore all those years.

My life is gone. Everything I had is gone.

Camille put a hand to her mouth and choked back another cry, unaware that the scrape left by Blackheart was now bleeding. Nausea ensued from all the commotion, and a wave of fatigue took over. She passed out, hearing the slight dripping of blood from her hand, just as another hunger cue rumbled in her stomach.

Hours later, she was awakened by an earth-shattering lightning bolt blast that illuminated the town and shook it worse than anything Blackheart had ever done. Light poured into all available cracks in the debris that surrounded her.

The whole world must have felt that.

She looked again at Anderson's body, and his eyes had still not left her. The ground settled, barely disturbing the ruins that shielded her from the outside world.

If I'm going to die, it won't be with him watching me.

Camille used all her remaining strength and crawled to Anderson's body. Each movement was more painful than the last. But she persisted and dragged herself closer, feeling the dirt become embedded in her wounds. The bruises became deeper, blood continued to flow out of her, but she persisted. She gritted her teeth and grunted as she continued onward.

She was utterly exhausted by the time she completed the ten feet to her former boss. She pulled herself up onto his ample stomach and clawed at anything around her to cover his face. She found a few broken bricks overhead and placed them over his eyes. They wobbled, but the dried blood coming from him acted as an adhesive to keep them in place.

I don't even want to know what he'd be saying if he knew that I was lying on top of him like this.

The nausea kicked in again, as did fatigue, and she lost consciousness.

She dreamed of eating. Not eating a meal but eating everything. A huge table around her with all the food she could imagine. Steaks, burgers, cookies, chocolate bars—nothing was forgotten or off limits. She gorged but just couldn't satisfy the hunger. And the more she ate, the hungrier she became.

Camille awoke to the sound of sirens. Her nose was buried into Anderson's bloodied and hairy chest, with some of the blood on her face. His smell was somehow better now than it was when he was still alive.

"Can anyone hear me!" a male voiced called out from beyond the remnants of Organic You's building.

The first responders are finally here! Oh, thank goodness! I may be able to make it out of this alive.

"Help! I'm in here!" she yelled weakly, straining her voice.

Her body was in such an injured and weakened state that she didn't have much time or energy left.

"Is there anyone here?" the voice called again.

"Please help me. I'm in here and I'm dying!" she eked out.

"I don't hear anything. How about over there?" the responder called to his colleagues, and Camille heard the sound of their boots leaving her area.

This can't be happening!

She was brought back to her current predicament as a fit of blinding hunger overtook her. It outweighed the worst of her injuries. It caused her to begin reasoning with herself.

How can I stand any type of chance if I don't have the energy to get help? Maybe just one bite. No one will ever know.

She was shocked by the thought. It wasn't an option. She didn't like eating certain cuts of steak, let alone another person. But she generally tended to be more of a meat eater. And that made this matter a bit easier to stomach.

It's either this or you're guaranteed to die. No one can hear you. It'll be weeks or even months before they find you at this rate. What do you have to lose? Who would even know? With all that fat on his body, I bet he's nice and tender. Like an undercooked pork roast.

Camille passed out again. She dreamed of nothing. Just darkness. And silence.

She woke up, already licking Anderson's blood off her face, even taking in some of his stray chest hairs. The blood was disgusting, with its iron-ridden funk, but it was some sort of sustenance. She felt like she was closer to death than ever before now. A fear worse than being inside that building when it fell. This was no longer resilience. This was survival. Her stomach cramped up, urging her to eat.

She looked up at Anderson again, who had begun to bloat and showed some mild signs of rigor mortis. His remaining skin was extremely discolored, and it appeared he evacuated his bowels at some point too. The bricks fell off his face, and now his eyes remained in position, still fixed on Camille.

Her stomach growled like a tiger in a pig pen. She lost control.

You were never nice to me. You never did anything for me. You can do this one thing for me on your way out, you fucking pig.

She bit off a gigantic chunk of his cheek, chewing and swallowing it quickly to avoid getting sick from the taste. She surprised herself and went back in again, eventually pulling his eyes out and dining on them too. The aqueous fluid was savory and no different than a warm glass of cream that had soured. His skin was softer than she expected, but the meat underneath quenched a deep hunger within.

You'll never make me feel uncomfortable ever again.

She felt satiated but then slightly sickened. As if her body were changing.

Am I too late? Is this what death feels like?

She went cold like it was the middle of winter as she swallowed one last bite of her former superior. She shivered and felt like she was about to vomit. Then the fatigue washed over her again. She wanted to try shouting for help one final time, but there were no more sirens or any indication of anyone left near her.

Camille gave up and lay down in the dirt, cuddling up to Anderson's legs. They felt so plump and primed that she felt hungry again. She dismissed the thought, already upset about what she had done to him. She prepared herself for death.

I know I've made a lot of mistakes. And I wasn't the nicest person. But for whatever it's worth, I know I could've been better. And I'm sorry to whoever I hurt during my life.

She was never one for prayer and didn't like organized religion, but it just felt right in the moment. She closed her eyes and died.

* * *

Camille was unaware of the change that happened after she passed away. Something foreign invaded her body, bringing new life. It manipulated her to rely on her base instincts. She grasped Anderson's legs and began to eat.

Chapter 3

In the nearby town of Mélange, Roger Todger sat in the Mélange Medical Center watching his wife, Katie, in her hospital bed. There were monitors all around her, her body a cacophony of tubes and wires. He leaned forward and kissed her hand, tasting some of the tape holding her IV in place. His brown eyes glistened with impending tears as his beautiful wife lay in peace, awaiting her imminent passing.

He thought of the first time they met, her angelic blue eyes, sandy blonde hair falling perfectly around her adorable face.

She spoke to him and said the most endearing thing. "Your parents really named you Roger Todger?"

He replied, "Yeah, they were very mean people."

It was the most amazing icebreaker that either of them ever experienced and was the catalyst for a loving, fulfilling, albeit brief, relationship.

He smiled at the memory, and the first tear dropped, landing on his pant leg. He stared at her face, thinking he would never see her again in her normal lively demeanor. Or looking up at him in the throes of passion. Or being silly. Or when she was mad at him and her cheeks got pink. The memories he had of her would be complete once she was no longer here. Their story would be over.

What started off as a suspected ovarian cyst turned out to be ovarian cancer that had already metastasized all over her body before they were able to get the first scan completed. She had spent the last two years in and out of surgeries in tremendous discomfort. And Roger was forced to sit there and watch all their efforts go to waste.

They both knew this would not end well. And it caused a lot of disagreements between them. He recalled one of the more recent arguments—

"We can go to a different oncologist. They may have something else we can try."

"No, Roger. I'm not going to a new doctor who isn't familiar with my history."

"So, you just want to let yourself die then? Not even try?"

"I'm fighting with every last bit I have, God dammit! Can't you see that?"

But neither of them was prideful. They were always quick to walk away from each other so as to not get too heated in the moment. And they would repair and reconnect—

"I'm sorry. I pushed too hard. I just love you too damn much to not do everything possible."
"But we are. We just have to put in the effort and hope things go our way. And if not, at least we tried our best."

They kissed and held each other in their favorite dark green armchair.

It wasn't too long after that when he came home from work to find her passed out on the kitchen floor. He shook her so violently, and she didn't respond. So he took her to the emergency room, and they informed him the cancer had progressed rapidly. They had no choice but to place her under palliative sedation to make her more comfortable until she died.

He took another deep breath, hoping desperately that a miracle would happen. That Katie would open her baby blues and stare lovingly back at him, telling him things would be okay.

"Please come back to me. I don't know what I'm going to do without you," he mumbled to her.

He then remembered dancing with her at their wedding, surrounded by loving friends and family, their lives ahead of them. Katie wore the classiest dress and looked like a dream. But it was her smile that he couldn't get over. It warmed his spirits, no matter how bad he felt. And she was so genuinely happy to just be with him. To commit herself to him for the rest of their lives.

They laughed and spun around on the dance floor and kissed each other passionately when the music ended as all their guests tapped their glasses. Roger had won awards in school, graduated college with honors, and received several promotions at work, but all it paled to the happiness he felt that day. The day that he married Katie. The love of his life.

Roger buried his hands into the bed next to her hand and didn't look up when a nurse entered.

"Mr. Todger, you should really get some sleep. We're doing everything we can for her right now," she said gently, placing a hand on his shoulder.

He looked up at her, seeing her name tag: Martha.

He replied solemnly, "I haven't slept in almost two years. A few more hours won't hurt."

The nurse rubbed his back briefly in a show of empathy before checking on Katie's vitals and leaving the room.

Roger just wanted to hold her one more time. To smell her hair, taste her lips, feel her skin, and hear her laughter. He wanted all of it back. He'd given up his entire life for her. Sacrificed larger promotions at work, left friends behind, all for her. It all hurt to do, but it was worth it. And he'd do it again if he could. Anything for his Katie.

Roger sat there for another hour before Katie's body began to squirm very slightly in the bed. Something was wrong.

He ran to the door and screamed for help. "My wife! There's something wrong with my wife! We need help in here!"

A small team of nurses ran in and asked him to stand outside. She was slipping away, and he couldn't even be in the room. He paced around the immediate area, feeling so helpless. He punched the wall in anger. Angry that she was in there without him.

"God, I'd give anything to have her be okay. Kill me instead and let her live," he said out loud, hoping God took him up on his offer.

There was no answer and no sign of the nurses to update him. He then heard the electrocardiogram transition from a steady beeping to the gentle humming of a flatline. Katie was gone. There was no more hope, no bargaining or anything else he could do. She was finally gone. He slumped against the wall, and his entire body crumbled inside and out. He wanted to cry but couldn't garner the needed energy to do it. He felt numb. The chaotic scene in the hospital went almost completely quiet as Roger became lost in his own mind.

I could've done more.
No, you did enough.
She should still be here, not you.
But she's gone and you're not.
You'll be alone forever now.
You will find peace again.

His thoughts were completely scrambled, and he couldn't focus. He felt like his brain and stomach had liquified. All those feelings and sensations were foreign to him. This was the first time he had suffered a major loss.

What am I supposed to do?

He felt that same gentle touch on his back again and snapped out of his funk to see nurse Martha again. Her red face and sad eyes told him exactly what she was about to say . . .

"Mr. Todger, I'm so sorry, but she's gone."

Roger's eyes closed, and more tears began to fall down his face. "I need to be with her right now," he requested, a totally broken man.

"Of course," Martha said, showing him complete empathy, walking him back to the room.

None of the staff members paid him any attention and were busy attending to other patients. Roger felt out of place, the only one showing any sign of distress, but he reminded himself these doctors and nurses did this all day, every day. They had become desensitized to certain feelings to keep themselves in check.

Roger stepped into the doorway, looking at the remaining two nurses removing all the medical equipment from the room. They moved quickly and tried not to look at him, out of respect.

"Please take all the time you need. We'll be right outside when you're ready," Martha said before walking out and gently closing the door.

It had been several days since he saw his wife's body without anything attached to it. She looked so peaceful. She was no longer in pain. He walked over to her on shaky legs and sat down, not taking his gaze off her.

He buried his hand within hers and just watched her. His heart had been torn out. He felt it. And that hole would remain there forever.

I'm so lost without you, my love.

He moved the chair closer and kissed her forehead, laying his head on her shoulder.

He tried to speak coherently, but the words just sputtered out. "I am going to miss you so much. I love you more than you could ever imagine."

And he broke down, letting it all out. While it was therapeutic, it still felt awful. But he needed to let it all out. He remained there for another hour until he was able to put himself together to go speak with the nurses about the next steps.

Chapter 4

Camille woke up inside a dark chamber.

This can't be the afterlife. It's so dark and cold. Where are the angels and fluffy clouds that we were all promised? What a rip-off.

Everything felt intact, even her legs. But even more so, she was filled with fear. She was trapped in this cold, pitch-black space.

I doubt heaven has metal like this.

She felt around, trying to get her bearings. She kicked against her surroundings and screamed, hoping someone heard her.

Faint voices and a weird clanking sound came from outside. Camille gave one final kick, jolting open a small door by her feet. Suddenly, light poured in, and she was able to push herself out. She stumbled to a standing position and saw an older gentleman, holding a half-eaten ham sandwich, and a younger man. They stopped dead in their tracks and just watched her. Their faces were full of fright and uncertainty.

"Where are my clothes? Where am I? Who are you!" she shouted.

"Is this some kind of a sick joke?" the older man asked his partner.

"I want some fuckin' answers. What have you done to me?"

"Ma'am, you're dead," the more senior of the two replied, trying to calm the situation.

"Don't you threaten me." Her voice deepened and her sense of self-control wavered.

"No, ma'am. My name is Gerald. This is my colleague, Simon. We are medical examiners at the Mélange Medical Center."

"What?" she continued to yell, completely confused. "What are you saying?"

"You were brought into the Mélange Medical Center several days ago. I personally evaluated your body, and you were deceased."

"Should I call security?" Simon asked, both men still unsure what to do.

"No, no. I think someone set us up. This is a joke. And a really convincing one too," Gerald assured him.

Camille realized she was totally naked and looked down at her body, which was stitched up all over. She noticed her nearby reflection and saw Mr. Anderson's eyes looking back at her. She looked down and saw his legs, which were now a part of her too. Whatever parts of him she had eaten became parts of herself.

What the hell is happening! This can't be real!

"Where are my parents? Why is no one here?" she yelled out, panicked.

"There were so many bodies taken out of Meadowsville after the incident there. The morgues and hospitals in all the surrounding areas pitched in. There just wasn't enough room. You were brought here. We didn't have a chance to identify you yet."

"Mélange?" She remembered him stating the name of the medical center earlier.

"Yes, ma'am. Now, can I please ask you to calm down so we can try to figure this out?"

Camille felt ravenous again, and the two men in front of her seemed more appetizing than they should have. Her sense of control now shifted to a dangerous place.

"Yes, I'll sit. Let's figure this out," she said calmly. "Now, can I have some clothes or are you two just enjoying the view?"

"Of course, I'm so sorry." Gerald scrambled to give her a lab coat.

Simon stared at her, blushing a bit.

She caught his glimpse. She began to rub her knees together and spread her legs, leaning back on a lab table, putting on a bit of show for her viewers.

Gerald looked unsure of her actions, as every part of her was attractive except for Anderson's large legs.

What's wrong with me? Why am I feeling this way? Why am I acting like this? I feel so different. But if he just comes a little closer, he'll be all mine.

Simon licked his bottom lip and stared at the discolored folds of her labia, becoming entranced. Camille heard a tear and her right inguinal fold split. She looked down and saw that her body had begun to come apart. She stood up, coming out of her seductive mindset, and the hunger took her over again. She couldn't control herself at all.

I can't wait for him. Must eat. Must fix it now.

A new voice in her mind started to gain access to her psyche. Something totally unknown. She noticed a female corpse a few feet away and ran to the body. Simon and Gerald were still stuck in place, watching the scene unfold. Camille pulled the plastic sheet off the body of a newly deceased woman. The toe tag read "Katie Todger." Camille stared the body down, envious of the pure vision of this woman, even in death.

The hunger made her lunge forward and bite on the woman's inner thigh, eating off the area she needed to repair. The taste was awful, resembling a cold slab of meat seasoned with chemicals, but she gulped it down. A few seconds later, she felt a slight sensation in her torn area. She looked down and the skin was now repaired, resembling the woman's skin and texture.

I absorb them. And become them. Whoever I eat.

Camille smiled at the epiphany with her canine-dominant teeth but was brought back to reality as she saw Mr. Anderson's chubby legs again.

No, no, no, we can't have that.

She looked at Simon and Gerald. Gerald finally dropped the sandwich he had been holding. He bolted out of the room, yelling for security, and Simon ran to the far corner of the morgue. Her time was now limited here, and she'd have to find a different source of body parts to keep herself alive.

That woman, Todger, didn't taste so bad after all.

Camille casually walked out of the room into a very plain hallway full of aged drop-ceiling panels and painfully worn white floor tiles. She continued down the corridor toward a side exit door and opened it, feeling the cool night sky. The slight breeze made each different body part feel unique—like having several different hands rubbing over each individual victim who had become part of her.

Chapter 5

"Roger, I'm so very sorry," his father-in-law, Franklin, said, pulling him in for a hearty hug in the main lobby of the Eternal Peace funeral home.

Marny, his mother-in-law, approached with a pained face and grabbed Roger before he could react. She smelled of expensive perfume, and he detected a slight hint of red wine on her breath. While he wanted to judge her, maybe she had the right idea to make getting through today a little easier.

"She loved you so much," Marny said in his ear, wiping some of her tears and snot on Roger's neck.

He didn't have the heart to say anything, so he just let the moment pass, staring hard at the maroon rug below them. She finally let go and went to her husband, and they entered the main area where Katie lay.

"My poor baby!" Marny yelled, falling into her husband's arms and causing a bit of scene in the viewing room.

Always one for the theatrics, Mom.

Roger had made a point to stay in the lobby, greeting everyone coming in so as to not be rude. He also was not prepared to see Katie's body. After being a part of several funerals for some of his distant family members, the bodies never looked right. Morticians had a really difficult job, making a decomposing corpse look like someone sleeping peacefully, so it wasn't like he expected her to look alive. But the bodies had been treated, made up, and chilled until the funeral. The mouths were glued shut, the skin looked like an odd fabric, the makeup made their features look ever so slightly off. While it looked like the deceased, the mind didn't let a person forget that it wasn't really them. It was just the shell of the person, but they were gone. And seeing his lost love in that state was going to be too much for him right now.

Roger never had any major setbacks or losses in his life. He didn't count distant relatives. The closest he came was when his pet hamster, Tater Tot, died, but he was never close with the animal. Katie was making him go through emotional turmoil he never could have prepared for.

It had been almost a week since her death, and the funeral was delayed due to the influx of bodies after the incident in Meadowsville. Roger spent each night driving past the funeral home, knowing Katie was inside, in that dark basement with some stranger seeing her naked form, poking and prodding. He even pulled into the small parking lot several times with the ambition of saving her and bringing her home. That was a crazy idea.

Or is it?

More of Katie's family came in, as did Roger's parents and some of their friends. Roger felt like he was on the brink of crying but just couldn't get there. He wanted to. He wanted to let it all out and allow his soul breathe a bit.

The funeral director, Robert, appeared out of nowhere like a ghost.

"Are you okay, Mr. Todger?" the large, pale man in an all-gray suit asked.

Roger nodded. The nod was an outright lie, but in a minute, he would be led to see his wife for the very last time.

"Okay then. It's time to start the ceremony." He gently led Roger into the room.

Roger's anxiety rose as a cold sweat broke out across his forehead. He took a deep breath and walked into the viewing room, seeing nothing but Katie's body from a few dozen feet away. She almost looked like herself from there. But it was just a body now. She wasn't actually there. Roger's heart sank once again as he now noticed the attendees, either crying or watching him enter the room from the various chairs and couches. No one was standing except him.

As he got closer, the noise in the room got quieter, and he entered his own personal bubble. He preferred it that way. He was never a big fan of large gatherings or being around huge numbers of people. This was no different. But this wasn't about him, and until that moment, he wasn't the center of attention. It was all for her. And Katie deserved everything.

Roger arrived at the coffin, seeing Katie in his peripheral vision as he stared straight ahead to the gorgeous picture collages and flower assortments everyone had brought. She loved roses and mums, and they were all freshly picked. The flowers were all white with some tasteful blue ribbons strewn upon them.

I have to look down, but I can't. I just can't do this. I'm not strong enough.

But it was time to see her. He looked down at his wife. She wore her favorite summer dress. A white fitted sleeveless top with a flared skirt. Even though her lower body was covered by the closed portion of the casket, he remembered how the playful sky-blue seashells danced around her lower body when she would wear it. Her hair was done to appear as if it were blown by the warm winds of the beach, off to her right shoulder. Her flawless porcelain skin... An internal combustion of emotions hit Roger, and he started crying uncontrollably as he finally looked at her face. It was just as he imagined. She looked like a cheap knockoff of his wife. It was like someone was playing a very terrible joke on him on the worst day of his life.

Who put pink lipstick on her? She hated pink lipstick!

He rested his elbows on the coffin and placed his head between his hands. She didn't smell anything like Katie either. He wanted his wife back so badly, even if just for a moment.

"I love you, Katie. Please come back to me," he bargained.

His parents, in their frail state, came to his side.

"She knows, my boy," Arnold told his son. "She knows."

His mom, Sophie, hugged him and kissed his head, taking him into her arms.

"I know this hurts. I can't imagine how much. Just let yourself feel it. Don't hold it in," Sophie told him.

But I don't know how!

Roger cried and didn't care if anyone got uncomfortable by his showing. He was confused and angry and completely displaced. His wife was dead. And he knew how all this worked. They would be here for him now. And maybe for a few weeks, but then they would be gone. The ones that stayed in contact would expect him to pull himself together after a while, or they would get tired of his depression and feelings and outright abandon him. And his parents had their own health issues, and travel was hard for them at this age. He wished they had decided to knock boots a decade earlier so they could be better able to be there for him better during a time like this.

But those thoughts were selfish. Even if true, this was the process with life. People were born and then they died. And if they were lucky, they would love someone as much as he did Katie or have someone love them equally. They all came here today to support him and be there in his time of need. And he needed to adjust his expectations.

The priest showed up late and stood at the flimsy podium, speaking some generic monologue, trying to link it to Katie. He didn't know her. Roger watched as the priest took a minute to look at her body as he uttered the word *beautiful*.

Don't look at my wife like that.

The priest stepped down—not soon enough—and everyone enjoyed each other's company, regaling each other with stories of Katie. Roger wanted to put on his faux chipper work persona and make some rounds to see everyone, but he didn't have the energy for it. He just wanted to sit there and be sad. He had nothing left inside to give to everyone right now.

But he enjoyed the togetherness and emotion involved with funerals, despite the crowds. It was so much different with someone who died and wasn't well-liked versus someone like Katie. These people all loved her and Roger, too, and were not here out of obligation.

He heard laughter and saw smiles among the tears, and the environment was welcoming and warming. Even if short-lived, he needed to take the time to appreciate it all.

His mother and father stayed at his side the entire time and made a point to keep saying nice and supportive things to him.

"We'll help you through this, honey. This storm is temporary and will pass."

"We love you, son. We're here for you."

These weren't just words but promises. And it meant a lot to him. And one by one, everyone came by and gave him hugs and encouragement.

Two hours went by, and Roger looked at his watch. Seven o'clock. It was time to wrap it all up now.

Roger stood up and walked to the lobby. Everyone noticed and took the subtle hint. Over the next twenty minutes, they all left. Their words to him upon their exits were placeholders.

Now was the true test of who would check in on him and still be a part of his new life.

"We'll call you when we get home, sweetie," Roger's mom said, caressing his cheek with her hand. "Do you need anything?"

Yes, bring her back for me.

Roger just felt numb. He didn't know what to do next but didn't want to inconvenience his parents.

"Thanks, Mom, but I'm okay for now. Just get to your flight and get home safely."

She hugged him one more time and so did his dad. They were such kind people, especially to their only son.

Roger turned to see the priest approaching him with a purpose. He knew what it was.

"Father Clark. Tom Clark." The priest offered his hand. "I'm so very sorry for your loss."

"Thank you, Father," Roger said, unimpressed.

"If you need anything, please call me." He handed Roger a business card. "Holy Name can be there for you. You're always welcome."

Roger's blood boiled a bit at the solicitation. Just another person who probably wanted to see how much life insurance money he got from his wife's death. All so he could just donate to a random church.

He quieted his mind and took the high road. "I appreciate that, Father. You'll be the first call I make," Roger said, unsure if he came across a little too sarcastically.

Then again, he didn't care if it was too insincere either.

Father Clark left the premises, and Roger was alone with the funeral director. Even after spending several hours here, Roger was amazed how such a large man could disappear and reappear so stealthily. He turned around, and the funeral director was looking down at him with soft features. Roger was still startled by this person strongly resembling Herman Munster.

"I'm sorry, Mr. Todger. I should have announced myself," Robert said.

"No, it's okay. Really. Today has just been a lot. But I'm sure you hear that often working here."

Robert nodded in agreement. "I believe all the pictures and flowers were taken by your guests. At your request?"

"Yes, the pictures were all doubles of ones I have, and I don't like flowers much. It's fine."

"Good. So you can take the guest book, if you'd like," Robert recommended as he closed the large leatherbound notepad, handing it to him.

Roger looked at it, fairly uninterested. Just as he told himself before, it didn't matter who was here. What mattered now was who would remain in his life moving forward.

"If it's okay, I'd rather not. I'm going to have so much to go through at the house, it'll just be another thing to find a place for," Roger said amicably.

"Very good, sir."

They stood in silence for a minute.

"She was the love of my life, Bob," Roger said gently.

"I know, sir. I could tell from the minute we first met."

Another moment of silence.

"If I may . . ."

Roger nodded.

"This is one of the hardest spots you'll ever experience. Grief is a devastating thing. And no two people go through it the same. So be gentle with yourself as you continue to go through the process. Your wife is no longer in pain and is waiting for you on the other side." Bob gently patted Roger's shoulder.

Roger smiled sincerely and valued his words. "Thank you, Bob."

They locked eyes momentarily.

"So, at this point, we'll take care of cleaning up and handling everything with the cremation. I'll call you in about a week or two so you can come collect Katie's cremains."

It struck Roger at that very moment how Katie would be burned. He had signed off on it, but it didn't occur to him until now what would actually happen to her. She was no longer alive, but the idea of it bothered him a great deal. He clenched his teeth and fists, tensing his whole body.

I can't let you burn. I won't let you burn. I'll be in that fire, if anything.

Bob noticed Roger's visceral reaction. "Go home and get some rest. My well-trained staff and I will take care of everything else for you."

Roger took another look in the viewing room at his wife. "Thanks again." He went to his car.

He usually liked to listen to the radio but left it off as he pulled out of the parking lot.

What kind of husband lets his wife burn? Go back there and save her, you idiot!

The insane thoughts ran through his mind, but as he got farther from the funeral home, they became sounder and more logical.

If anyone chooses what happens to her body, it should be you. You sacrificed everything for her. And she was worth it. She'd want the same. This doesn't need to be the last time. You can bring her home. To her home. With you.

Roger stopped the car in the middle of an intersection—luckily, there was no one else near him—then he sped back to Eternal Peace. The front door was still open, and the cleaning staff was working. Katie's body was still in the coffin.

"Katie, you're coming home with me." He got out of the car and walked back inside to his wife.

The cleaning staff stopped vacuuming and dusting, unsure of his intentions. He must have looked dangerous to them, as their faces were all fearful.

"I'm not going to hurt you. This is my wife. And she's coming home with me."

Roger felt crazy as he opened the casket base and readied himself to pick her up. Her body was cold and stiff and weighed almost double after being treated by the mortician. Roger thanked himself for staying in such good shape over the years.

He hoisted her into his arms as he remembered carrying her over the threshold after their wedding. Her dress rode up slightly, and he noticed an area near her groin that was heavily patched up. He wondered what the injury was from. He smiled, not caring what anyone thought of his outrageous actions.

The cleaning staff stayed put, not making a move of any kind.

But the funeral director ran down from his office, yelling out, "Roger, you can't do that. There are laws we must follow. She is in better hands here!"

Roger, beginning to fatigue at the weight of Katie's body, turned to Bob. "Then call the cops. Get me arrested on the worst day of my life. See if I give a shit," Roger snarled.

He then settled himself. Bob was just doing his job.

"You keep the money for the cremation. All you have to do is keep your mouth shut. I'm taking my wife home with me."

* * *

Bob watched Roger gently place Katie in the backseat of his car and drive off. He, too, was amazed at Roger's feat of strength.

"Jesus fucking Christ almighty in the highest. I need a drink," he said to himself. He turned back to his staff, telling them to keep cleaning.

Bob returned to his office and never breathed a word about Roger's actions.

Chapter 6

Camille found herself in the Holy Name Catholic Church cemetery, which was roughly the size and landscape of several football fields, with about twelve hundred bodies per acre. She couldn't understand why, but this place had summoned her to be there.

Things were different now. She was weaker than normal and wanted only to sleep and eat. Her body was functioning on a purely instinctual level. Each minute she was in this new form, another chunk of her memory and personality diminished. Some pieces were gone, while others remained.

She didn't remember her middle name. Or where she used to work. But she remembered Mr. Anderson, whose eyes now functioned as her own.

She crawled on top of a crypt. Using her adopted legs from Anderson proved to be the hardest part of the climb. They were heavy and troublesome to maneuver. She fell into a deep sleep for several hours before awakening. She was hungry and leered across the graveyard at a funeral procession coming to a close. All the people there, dressed in black, walked away as the casket was being buried by a single gravedigger. She could see his frizzy red hair and matching handlebar mustache. Each movement allowed a single drop of sweat to fall off his face.

Time to eat. You need to eat.

Camille descended from the crypt, creeping toward the gravedigger as she used large tombstones to camouflage herself. The late afternoon sky was beginning to turn to dusk, and she smelled scotch from the panting worker. She got closer and closer, realizing she wasn't strong enough to attack a live victim. If she ate enough body parts, that might change. But she wasn't sure.

I wish that I knew what the hell I was and how this worked.

Her instincts kicked in, and she leapt out a mere foot from the worker, screaming at the top of her lungs. The sound didn't come out so much a scream but rather an unnatural screech. Her mouth snapped shut and her sharpened teeth cut into her bottom lip, but no blood came out.

Guess I need to fix that now too.

The digger dropped his shovel and jogged off haphazardly from his recent drinking. "I fuckin' knew this job was a bad idea. I'm outta here!" he yelled upon his sprint out of the graveyard.

Camille licked her now severed lower lip and felt something underneath. A very rough texture, as if there was something else beneath her patchwork of skin and body parts.

What happened to me in Meadowsville? Why didn't I stay dead?

Camille wanted to feel fearful of whatever was happening to her, but it was becoming easier to live like this.

She dove down onto the partially buried coffin. Her heavy Anderson legs fractured the lid and gave her almost immediate access to the body.

Just a little dirt. I can handle that.

Much to Camille's delight, it was a rather slender middle-aged woman. She scoped the body to see what the legs looked like, both of which were intact. She was careful not to ruin the clothes, which she would use for herself. The pants were guaranteed to fit once she finished dining on this woman's legs. The left knee had scarring, possibly from a knee replacement, but it didn't matter much.

Let's get rid of these thunder thighs, and then we'll worry about the eyes. These ugly, bothersome eyes.

She noticed how her biting and chewing abilities were far beyond what she had as a human, despite the rest of her body being somewhat frail. The legs tasted like moisturized jerky, but she swallowed them down with ease.

Camille stood tall atop the coffin, waiting for her legs to change. Slowly, the skin shifted and took on their new form. It tingled a bit but was not an unpleasant sensation.

Some dirt fell from the sides of the hole on her bare feet. She peeled the muddied blouse and skinny jeans off her prey and put the pants on her now almost perfect legs.

Goodbye, Anderson, you fat slug.

Camille realized the cemetery would be the easiest place for her to find body parts to keep herself from falling apart, so she should stay put. At least until she had a better knowledge of what type of creature she had become.

Chapter 7

"Okay, mental checklist. Scale, laptop, patient files, water bottle. Check, check, and double check." Roger put on his backpack, tightening the straps so there was no slack.

His blood pressure cuff and stethoscope were packed away in a handy black fanny pack. His short-sleeved black polo wrinkled a bit at the abdomen, but he straightened it out. He readied himself to start another day of work at Tick Tech Logistics.

He had worked as a wellness coach for fifteen years. His background was in exercise physiology, a specialized healthcare discipline. Roger always imagined himself working in a cardiac rehab unit at some major hospital, but those jobs were hard to come by. And they didn't necessarily pay much. But his job at DPS Health allowed him to work at his own pace, and he didn't have a boss looking over his shoulder every two minutes to tell him something wasn't up to their standards. DPS contracted him and his colleagues to various sites across the country, and as wellness coaches, they acted as the on-site health and wellness coordinators. They reviewed preventative lifestyle factors with the employees, including diet, exercise, and sleep hygiene, all aimed at not only improving their quality of life by reducing risk factors for chronic illnesses but also saving the organizations money on insurance premiums. So it was a really solid mission—and Roger, despite never knowing this type of job existed before working in it, flourished.

Roger approached the first cubicle and focused on staying present, trying not to think about Katie's body in his basement. He was petrified someone would break into his house and see her. He was less worried about them taking something and much more concerned about something happening to the body.

"Roger Todger!" the man called to him, spinning around in his desk chair.

"Hey, Charlie! How are you feeling today?" Roger responded, snapping into his happy-go-lucky work self.

"I'm good. Hey, man, I'm so sorry to hear of your loss. You hangin' in?"

Roger took a breath, thinking of Katie again. "Yeah, I'm doing okay. Just taking things day by day."

"That's good," Charlie said. "Hey, you like my new ergonomically sound chair?"

Roger feigned interest. "I love it! Definitely should help with your hip discomfort. Have you had a chance to try some of those corrective movements I emailed to you last week?"

Charlie stared at Roger blankly. "Oh no, I haven't yet. Sorry about that. Things have just been so busy here. We sold a ton of these newly developed graphics cards. Kids are eating them up."

"I get it. Well, let's see how the chair impacts it and definitely try those exercises out. Should make you right as rain."

"You got it, bud. And hey, thanks for being here. We all figured that you would have taken a few weeks off work. To, ya know, take care of everything."

Roger always hated when people pried. He did his best to redirect the conversations, but it wasn't easy with some people.

"Nope, I have it all under control. But again, keep me posted on your hips, and good luck doing the entries for those graphics cards."

"Have a great day, Roger!"

"You, too, Charles." Roger collected himself for a few seconds as he went to the next cubicle.

The middle-aged woman sat with her back to him, shopping for new shoes online. It always made Roger laugh to himself when the employees complained that they had no time to do their work but always seemingly had time to check their social media accounts and shop during the workday.

"Maryanne, how are you feeling today?"

God, this woman can talk. Each person gets two to five minutes. Not forty-five!

She spun in her chair and looked Roger up and down.

Ick!

"Well, look at you, dear," she said, grabbing his right hand. "We were all so sorry to hear about Katie. She was a beautiful girl. But you'll be okay. Just give it time."

Roger hated the words, even if they came from a good place. "I appreciate that, Maryanne. So how are you today? How have your sugars and blood pressure been?"

"My sugars were a little up last night. My goddamn—" She motioned to herself to lower her voice. "My goddamned husband keeps sneaking these cookies in the house. The ones with the mint chocolate center. I don't even know what they're called, but I just can't stop myself."

God, I hope Katie's body is okay.

"I totally understand. That must be really challenging. So, in past instances, you've shared with me how you would buy some lower-calorie snacks to take care of that sweet tooth. Was that still something you might want to do to combat the cravings?"

Maryanne nodded. "Roger, you're right. I almost forgot about that. I can't believe you remember that from all those years ago. Those little one-hundred-calorie packs are perfect."

"Okay, great. So when's the next time you're headed to the store, so we can put the plan into action?"

SMART goals . . . specific, measurable, achievable, relevant, time-bound. Just give me a day, Maryanne, so we can wrap this up.

Maryanne's cell phone vibrated and moved the pile of papers underneath it.

She stopped their conversation and looked. "Oh, honey, this is my chiropractor. I have to take this. Can you check my pressure while I'm on the call?"

Just what I wanted to do, Maryanne. Check your pressure while you talk too loud on your phone.

"Sure thing," Roger said, faking excitement to do so.

He positioned the cuff, found the brachial artery, and evaluated her pressure. The Korotkoff sounds made him think of napping on Katie's stomach, listening to her heartbeat. Then it quickly turned into the memory of her being hooked up to all those monitors in the hospital before she died. He sniffled and felt the sweat build up across his hairline, but Maryanne didn't hear over her loud voice.

She then rudely held up a blood pressure tracking card for him to write down, without looking at him again. He wrote down the accurate reading of 130/78 and gave her a thumbs up as he left her area.

Thank God I only have to do that another one hundred and thirty-three times today. MDs, eat your heart out.

Roger listened to many more staffers bringing up Katie, and he just wanted the day to end. Knowing she was home, where she belonged, was enough motivation to take the onslaught of employees more tolerable.

The next six hours went by quickly, and Roger sat in his car, mentally and physically fatigued. He hadn't sat since he first put on his gear that morning. Even with the emotional and physical toll it took, he loved his job immensely and enjoyed helping people. But he went to work each day to help everyone else with their problems. And they rarely ever asked him how he was.

Do they even care? Why did it take Katie dying for them to finally give a shit?

And a good deal of the time, people just talked *at* him, sharing obvious inaccuracies they bought into. For instance, they'd found some new miracle drug to help them lose the twenty pounds they put on since the prior year. The exercise and diet fads changed so often that it was hard to keep track of sometimes. The Organic You company was something he heard about nonstop for the last year and made his blood boil. He couldn't believe how many people were willing to go against proven treatments for health-related concerns. All because they thought they knew better.

Not my problem. I'm there to help them make decisions for themselves. Not make decisions for them. Whether they're the right decisions or not is on them.

He was there to be an informative support. If they asked him for recommendations, he would give it to them, but otherwise, he was there to guide each individual in their own journey. And it was satisfying, not as an ego boost for himself but just to help someone live a better life. To give them purpose and motivation to do something to benefit themselves. He just wished someone did that for him.

Like at the funeral—all that love and support. He missed it. He needed it. And without it, he couldn't be present or in the right mindset for his patients at work. Or be there for himself. And more important, Katie.

Stop thinking of her like she's alive.

Roger drove home in complete silence for the next hour, thinking of nothing but seeing his wife and going to bed. He had four more days after this until the weekend. Maybe he should've taken off more than a week to situate himself after Katie died. The company allowed for more, but part of him just wanted to get back into his normal routine. Or whatever the new normal would look like.

He unpacked his bags and went down to the basement. There was nothing else to do since he was the only one in his house now. No sweeping, no dishes, and nothing different than when he left eight hours ago.

He had Katie in a small storage area off his finished basement. It was nice and cool in there and would be the best way to preserve the body. He opened the door and looked at his bride. Roger smiled, but his heart was heavy in the moment. The odor of decay was present, but he ignored it. It was a small price to pay to be in her presence again.

Roger's curiosity got the better of him, and he lifted Katie's dress to see the wound that he noticed at the funeral home. It had a ton of product on it and looked almost like teeth marks.

"What the fuck did that to you, sweetie?" he asked Katie.

Part of him hoped she would jump awake and everything would be normal again. Like she was never sick and didn't suffer and was just there as only she could be. But nothing happened.

Roger fixed her dress and noticed that a few of her toes were rotting off. He didn't know a thing about preserving a body but needed to learn now. It was that or watch her deteriorate all over again. Only this time, it would be the definitive last time.

Roger rushed to his nearby laundry room and pulled out his tiny sewing kit. He was in a frenzy to fix her body. He threaded the needle in record time and went to Katie's right foot. Her great toe was in bad shape, but he was willing to try anything.

"I'm sorry, hon. I'll be quick," he said, proceeding to sew the toe back in place.

Each time he punctured her skin, the feeling of regret weighed strongly on his mind. He finished up, and it was a little lopsided, but it would do for now. She just needed a new toe, as her current one was barely salvageable. But where could he get it?

Then he had a diabolical idea.

Chapter 8

Roger woke up even earlier than normal the following morning. He turned on his laptop and searched the local obituaries. He had gotten only about four hours of sleep, which he'd became very used to while caring for Katie during her illness. He was doing major damage to his body without getting in at least six hours a night, but he had work to do. Katie needed him. He scanned Google's search results and saw several write-ups but needed something more specific. He wanted someone younger to match the body parts to. Everything he saw were older adults that just wouldn't be compatible.

Here I am at the ripe age of thirty-seven, looking at toe donors. What a path I've chosen for myself.

And there it was—

Carrie O'Sullivan Beloved mother and wife. Passed away suddenly from cardiac-related complications at the age of forty-four in her sleep. Born and raised in

Mélange, she excelled in her schooling and was the youngest assistant manager at Elite Petroleum. She enjoyed fishing, hiking, and playing her guitar. She is survived by her husband, Donald, and two daughters, Danielle and Summer. Visiting hours will be at the Heirloom Funeral Home from 2:00 to 4:00 p.m. and 5:00 to 7:00 p.m. on May 23. Per the family's request, donations can be made to the Heart Foundation.

Well, she's a little older than Katie, but a toe is a toe. No one will notice if I leave work a little early today.

Roger packed a suit in his car and left for work after kissing Katie on the forehead. His lips stuck a tiny bit to her eroding skin, but he looked beyond it at her deformed toes.

"I'll make it right, honey. Don't you worry about a thing," he told her with a smile.

Roger spent most of the workday a prisoner in his own mind but got through it, feeling a bit more energized than he had in some time. He left work about forty-five minutes early to make it to the second viewing. He parked about a block away and quickly changed into his suit in the backseat of his car. He was very appreciative of his tinted windows at a time like this.

He got himself ready and entered a crowded event almost an hour late, which was good. He could blend in and not be noticed as an outsider.

He looked around, and no one acknowledged him. He walked in the viewing room, looking past all the people and on to Carrie O'Sullivan. A flashback of Katie lying in her casket overtook his mind, but he shook it off.

He walked toward the coffin, trying to make sure Carrie's body was intact, at least enough to take a few toes. He looked down at Carrie, and much like Katie, she had a very artificial appearance. A hand slapped him on the back, and he turned to see a stout, grief-stricken man. He was red in the face but had a small, forced smile.

"I thought I knew everyone here, but I don't think we've met, son," the man said with a slight Southern accent.

Roger thought it was strange to hear someone else call him *son* besides his father.

"I'm Roger." He wanted to kick himself for using his real name.

"Hi, Roger, I'm Donald."

Both turned to look at Donald's late wife.

"I always thought I'd be the first one gone. That woman needed more time on this earth," Donald said, wiping his tears.

Roger felt himself back at work. There to help someone else with their feelings.

"I know, Donald. If I hadn't just lost my wife recently, too, I wouldn't say a thing to you," Roger expressed empathetically. "But I understand."

"Oh gosh, you, too, huh?" Donald replied. "What was it, if I can ask?"

Roger swallowed hard. "It was ovarian cancer. A long two-year battle, and she lost."

Donald slapped his back again and pulled him in for a hug. Roger started to feel the calming fulfillment here with these strangers that he had at Katie's funeral.

"Oh, I'm sorry to hear of it. I just don't understand how this goddamned world works sometimes. It takes good people away and leaves so many good-for-nothings hanging around."

Roger nodded, genuinely agreeing with the statement. He couldn't figure out why Katie was taken so soon either. And he didn't agree with whatever reasoning there might have been.

Donald looked over Roger's shoulder and saw his two daughters being consoled by his sister.

"Listen, Roger. Thank you for coming today," Donald said, starting to cry more. "My poor kids don't have a mother anymore. And I don't know if I can do this alone."

Roger felt for this poor man, even beyond his own selfish intentions for being at this event. And while he and Katie lost a few pregnancies, he was glad in that moment that they never had children. They were trying for a third time, but that soon turned into the first symptoms of Katie's cancer, which they thought was some sort of complication at first. Sadly, it wasn't so simple. But, needless to say, being a single father with a work schedule like his was not a good match.

Roger focused hard to stay in the moment and spoke to Donald tactfully. "Donald, I know we just met. And it's awful to be under these circumstances. Carrie was a damn fine lady, and we were all lucky to have known her."

"How did you know my wife anyway?"

"Work." Roger defaulted to the obituary. "We worked together at EP for a few months. I'm sorry I didn't get to know her better."

Donald looked to Roger for more.

"She always spoke about you, Danielle, and Summer." Roger said, recalling the funeral listing details. "You guys were the world to her."

Donald took out a handkerchief and blotted his eyes.

"And those kids are lucky to have you as a daddy. And look at all the supportive people here for you guys." Roger guided Donald to look around the room. "You'll figure it out. All of it. And you'll come out a better man on the other side. I know it. You got this."

Roger had always been good at quickly reading people and being able to communicate efficiently with them. He had almost a sixth sense about it, which was why he was so efficient at his job.

Donald nodded and slapped Roger's shoulder for a third time, with Roger almost wincing in pain.

"Thank you. I needed to hear those words," he replied with a crimson face.

They both looked at Carrie again, which made Roger again feel guilty for his true purpose there. But he had to do it, or he'd be letting Katie down.

"Well, Roger, you keep in touch, and I hope to get a beer with you sometime," Donald said to his new friend, shaking his hand and walking away to see more attendees coming in.

"Wow, that was really something," Roger heard through the noise directly behind him.

He turned to see a woman sitting by herself in the front row of chairs. She had on a relatively conservative loose-fitted black dress. She wasn't smiling but seemed rather intrigued by Roger.

She stood up and shook his hand. "You were really good with Donald. He's such a nice person. This is awful for him and the girls."

"Yeah, he seems so. But he'll be okay."

"I'm Allison Miller, an old friend of Carrie's. We lost touch, but I had to be here to pay my respects. And you're Roger, right?"

Roger smiled politely and nodded.

"Do you have a last name, Roger?" she asked of him.

"Todger. My name is Roger Todger," he spat out.

Allison stifled a laugh and put her hand over her mouth.

"I know. My parents were really mean people," Roger said, smiling and finally making eye contact with her.

He felt strange speaking with another woman like this, and it was very uncomfortable using one of the first things he said to Katie with her too. But he hadn't been on a date in over a decade, so he didn't know anything beyond what his already established verbal skills consisted of.

Allison smiled and chuckled, which put Roger at ease. "So, I'm sorry to hear about your wife. When did it happen?"

"About a week ago."

Her eyes grew in amazement. "Oh my God. I thought you meant it was a while ago. Why are you here and not home?"

"I wanted to pay my respects to Carrie. And I needed to get out of the house too. Gets lonely sometimes."

"And a funeral is your first option, huh?" she teased a bit.

"I dunno. Funerals are a nice spot. It's the celebration of the end of someone's journey. And you see everyone being genuine. Nothing fake here. You see people for who they really are. With their guards let down. Just a nice change of pace, ya know?" Roger replied.

"I never thought of it that way. But that was deep and insightful, Mr. Todger." Allison said. "So you said you knew Carrie from work?"

Roger was unsure how to field her question.

Shit, shit, shit.

"Sort of. I'm a health-care contractor. I was stationed at her EP office for a few months, but the contract wasn't renewed."

"So, what is your background in?"

"Exercise physiology. But I work as a wellness coach."

She looked at him like he had three heads, totally confused. "What's that? Like a personal trainer?"

Roger couldn't help but laugh out loud. A few of the other guests looked over at him, and he put his hand up as a nonverbal apology.

"No, not like them at all. It's an actual discipline and specialized field in health care. We are trained to fully understand how the body works and combine that with exercise science. And we use that to work with people on using physical activity to improve their health and performance, reduce risk factors, manage injuries, and other stuff like that."

"Wow, sounds interesting. I had no idea that even existed," she replied.

"We're still a small field. And what do you do?"

"Nothing half that unique. I'm a purchasing agent for city hall. Lots of phone calls to vendors, pricing out contractors, processing work orders, and paperwork galore."

Roger and Allison looked at each other, feeling very comfortable in the conversation. It turned out Allison had grown up in Mélange, just as Roger did, but they were a few years apart in school. She'd been working at city hall since she graduated and had a nice, comfortable position there. They spoke about Katie a bit, and Roger became a little emotional, but Allison didn't push the issue too much. They continued speaking for a while longer before the funeral director started to shoo people out the front door.

Both stood up and looked at each other, unsure of what to do.

"Listen, Roger. I really enjoyed this. I know it's a little strange meeting someone at a funeral."

"Stranger than Mr. Humphries in ninth-grade English class?" he said, referencing an old teacher they both had.

The man had a Miss Piggy doll behind his desk that he would strangle every time he got anxious. Roger had thought it was a running joke until he saw the doll. The thing looked like a sick giraffe.

"A little bit," she replied, smiling. "But I'd like to keep in touch. Would that be okay?"

Roger felt a wave of anxiety, feeling like he just cheated on Katie somehow. Allison noticed his hesitation and told him it was okay, then turned away.

"No, no." He stopped her. "That'd be nice. I'd like to stay in touch with you too."

What are you doing?

They put each other's names and numbers in their cell phones and shook hands again.

"It was nice to meet you, Roger Todger." She lingered a bit.

"And you, too, Allison Miller." He watched her walk to her car.

Roger hung back after everyone left and snuck to the downstairs of the funeral home, where the mortician would be. It was behind a large metal door and looked exactly as cold and impersonal as one would imagine. Everything smelled of bleach and was shiny metal, with matched tables, instruments, and storage freezers.

"Hello," Roger called out.

A toilet flushed and a bald older man came out of a back room. He looked unsure of Roger's presence.

"Can I help you?"

"Hi, my name is Bill," Roger lied, shifting side to side.

"Yeah, I'm George," the mortician hesitantly said.

"George, I have a bit of a strange request and was wondering if you could help me."

The man crossed his arms and demonstrated a surly face towards Roger.

You got this!

"If I needed to obtain something very specific from your office, how would that work?"

George looked at him genuinely confused. "We only have bodies and instruments down here. I don't sell nothing. Not really sure what you're gunning at either. But let's get to the point. It's late and I want to leave."

Roger tensed up, doubting his ability to close the deal with George. He put his hand into his jacket pockets and pulled out $5,000, which he had withdrawn from the bank when Katie's ample life insurance policy came through. And surprisingly, it was processed very quickly. He slapped it on the metal preparation table.

"You may want to hear me out," Roger pushed.

George nodded and walked to a small desk in the far corner of the room. He took something out of the top drawer, but Roger couldn't see what it was. He hid it behind his back and slowly walked back to Roger.

"Listen, pal. I don't let people fuck the bodies or anything. You want to do something like that, go find another funeral home. This is all legit here," George said angrily.

He's got a weapon. Get out of here!

"No, nothing like that," Roger assured George. "I just require maybe a piece of two of some or your bodies. You can take 'em off. I won't touch anything. That's it."

George lost his patience and spit on the ground, pulling a small revolver out from behind his back. Roger quickly grabbed his money and backed away with his hands up.

"Get the fuck out of here, you creep. You want body parts and shit. Get outta here before I call the cops. *Now!*"

Roger ran upstairs and out the front door, racing to his car and slamming the door. He tossed the money into the passenger seat.

"Fuck, this is going to be harder than I thought." He tried to catch his breath.

Time isn't on your side either. She's rotting more and more each day. You gotta move your ass.

Roger leaned on the headrest, knowing he'd have to risk this type of thing again before he found a mortician willing to help.

He wiped the sweat from his brow and started the car. "Guess tomorrow will be another adventure."

He sped off into the night.

He needed body parts and needed them fast.

Chapter 9

The following day at work, Roger sat on a conference call with his operations manager, Tom. He was a good man who knew Roger was on top of his game at all times and rarely, if ever, missed a deadline or report or needed to be ridden to do an efficient job. There was a nice mutual respect, and not a day went by that didn't see Roger humbled and appreciative of his job.

"So, Roger, how are you holding up?" Tom's voice came in a little staticky.

Roger leaned back in the rickety executive chair in the otherwise empty office. Since he floated site to site each day, Roger had no official space. He just worked out of whatever open spots he could find on a given day.

"I'm doing okay," he responded. "Starting to clean out Katie's stuff from the house little by little. It's a process, ya know?" Also, a blatant lie.

Tom was quiet for a few seconds. "Understood. Well, take your time with it and if you need any more time off . . . I know you depleted your paid time off when she was sick, but we can work with you to figure something out. No pressure, but the offer is there. We care about you and want to make sure you're good."

The other thing Roger enjoyed about his manager was how genuine and low pressure he was. So the sincere words felt good to hear. Even though he knew all this already, it was nice to hear the words reinforced.

"Thank you, Tom, I appreciate that."

"So how are your sites? Your reports all look good. Stable participation. Site contacts are happy. We never have to worry about you, Roger. Always a true blue, as the old expression goes."

Roger smiled and felt the same good feelings he got from being around funerals. Supportive and appreciated.

"Do you have any special programs coming up? Did you reach out to the insurance broker to see if you can help them with any initiatives for the staff?"

"Yep, running a hydration promotion program in July. The insurance broker never responds to me, honestly, but I did reach out to them a few times. I don't want to keep bugging them. You know the drill, Tom."

Tom laughed a bit and agreed. "Unfortunately, I do. They're so inconsistent, but they give us a lot of business. So no worries. I appreciate you keeping me in the loop."

They both sat on either end of the phone in quiet.

"I guess we can keep this quick, as always. Again, if you need anything, please let me know. We're here for ya, Roger. All of us here at HQ."

Yeah, I need something. A couple toes and a consistent flow of body parts to keep my dead wife's body intact.

"Will do, Tom. Thanks for taking the time to jump on a call. I know how busy you are."

They ended the call, and Roger looked at the clock. Time for him to head over to the His and Hearse Funeral Home. Roger decided, after the bad experience last night, he'd try to see the mortician at this event when there was a large group present. They would be less likely to attack him with witnesses around. And he found four funerals today, but this place had the classiest—note the sarcasm—name. Any mortician willing to work there must not be too strict with their practices.

Upon his arrival, he saw the funeral home was small and sported a lighted sign out front reading *We put the fun back in funeral*. A steady flow of people walked in. They were all dressed in dark colors, and it seemed a little less inviting than Carrie O'Sullivan's funeral. Not many smiles or comradery. Everyone just sort of marched in one after another.

When Roger walked in, there was a short, fidgety funeral director who had his tie on cockeyed and wore a nametag that read *Hi, my name is Herbert. We urn our business.* Roger shook his head in disgust at the strange puns.

Who the hell would come to a place like this?

The lobby was a bit messy, with lots of steel folding chairs and little tables holding various business cards of local vendors, pamphlets of the funeral home's services, and other materials. The entire place reeked of a sales pitch.

Roger entered the viewing room, which took up a good part of the building, filled with chipped and scratched wooden chairs on beige carpet leading up to the body of today's corpse, Faith Lindsey.

I never liked when people have two first names like that.

The walls and ceiling were not in stellar shape, showing an aged off-white color.

Seeing the body filled him with anxiety, possibly from this being his third funeral in a week's time. He was becoming desensitized to the presence of dead bodies, but it was still uncomfortable. And he was sure sewing his wife's rotted toes back on probably contributed a bit too.

When he had checked on his wife before leaving for work that day, her hands were starting to discolor greatly, and other parts of her appearance too. It was like watching a gorgeous flower wilt, with nothing left but rotted petals on a barren ground.

Roger looked at Faith's wrinkled face—she had been seventy-nine years old when she passed. She looked like a kind woman, and even though her body parts would not be a good match for Katie, something was better than nothing at this point. His wife needed him.

Roger also was surprised by how well-preserved and lively her appearance was.

This must be some talented mortician to do work this good.

He walked around the viewing area, looking at the pictures of Faith with her family and friends over the years. The woman in the photos never smiled and had a constant look of aggravation on her face.

Very unlike the lady in the casket with her peaceful smile and gentle features. *I guess appearances can be deceiving.*

Roger took a seat in the very back of the room, trying to find someone to strike up a conversation with. A strong majority of the guests were much older than him, so this would be a tall task. An older woman sat next to him and gave a brief smile. Everyone started to take their seats in preparation for Faith's husband, who would be conducting the eulogy.

"How did you know Faith?" Roger asked the older woman.

She didn't respond, so he assumed she didn't hear him.

"Ma'am. Hi, I'm Roger. How did you know Faith?" he asked again.

She turned her head and responded, "We were neighbors for many years."

He nodded and tried to make up a believable story if she asked him the same question. "How did she pass?"

"It was sudden. Her son was one of the victims of the Meadowsville incident, and she died shortly after hearing the news of his passing. Sad story," the old woman explained.

There's my in!

"How did you know Faith?" the woman asked Roger.

Roger was distracted by the sniffles of a few guests around him. He once again took great comfort in the solemn vibe in the room. It matched the way he felt on the inside. Even though this was a little more of a more conservative crowd, he enjoyed the environment.

"Roger?" she asked again.

He snapped out of his thoughts, "Oh, sorry. I was a friend of her son's. I didn't know Faith very well, but I wanted to be respectful."

She nodded just as Faith's husband began to speak about his wife. He spoke with very little emotion in a deep, monotone voice. His words came across in a superficial way, a bit forced, and not because he meant any of it. Roger suddenly felt out of place, very unlike his experience at Carrie O'Sullivan's event.

Where is the love here? Why is it all so cold?

Roger excused himself to go find the mortician.

He passed the funeral director, who was in his office on his desktop computer, paying no attention to the ceremony, and found the stairway leading down to the mortician's area. The hallway had almost no lights, and the stairs had a subtle stickiness to them, which he hoped was not from any bodily fluids.

Gosh, this place gets worse and worse.

Roger passed a license plate hanging in the hallway that read *I-MBALM* and a small sign directly above the door reading *My day starts when your day ends*, both of which made him chuckle. As he faced the metal door, he knocked and waited for a response.

A smaller man with crooked glasses and an oddly parted hairdo opened the door and scrunched his nose at Roger. "Yes," he asked.

"Hi, my name is . . . uh . . . well, let's just call me RT," Roger said.

The man looked unsure and didn't take his hands off the door. "Okay, RT, what do you want?"

Roger couldn't get a read on this person. "I'd like to speak with you about a proposition."

The man smiled and softened his facial features. "A proposition, huh? I get it. You wanna come in here and fuck some dead bodies, right?"

What the hell is wrong with this guy?

Roger quickly shook his head and took a step back. "God, no, that's not it at all."

The man put his hand up to calm Roger and opened the door. "Hey, man, I'm just kidding. Come on in, partner." He guided Roger in.

Roger was completely uncomfortable and not sure what he'd gotten himself into. The man was not dressed like other morticians. He had faded blue jeans on, torn up at the knees, and a shirt that read *Morticians aren't like corpses. We're just stiff in all the right places.*

Roger giggled a bit, still completely uncomfortable, as they walked into the main preparing area. There are several bodies lying out that the mortician was working on. One body had a book lying across the abdomen titled *Yetis, Sasquatches, and Bigfoot.* The man jumped up and sat next to the corpse of an older woman.

"Okay, so talk. What can I help ya with?" The man removed his glasses and wiped the lenses with his shirt. "These are just for show. Makes me look smarter. Kidding."

Roger smiled and warmed to this man's quirkiness. "So I'm looking for some privileges here. I need to acquire some body parts." Roger just came out and said it. "I'm sorry, I didn't get your name, by the way."

The man looked at him and then grabbed a nearby glass full of whiskey, taking a small sip. "Well, since we're not using real names, I want something that sounds tough. Something cool. Something smooth." He looked down at the glass again. "Just call me Mr. Whiskey. No bullshit nicknames like Whisker, Whisk, or Corpse Cuddler, okay? These people are dead, but I'm not. I got feelings, RT. You got me?"

Is this guy joking? I honestly can't tell with anything he's saying.

The more Whiskey spoke, the smoother his delivery of each line was. Each sentence began blending into the other.

"Okay, RT. Let's talk shop. I got something you need. Now, what's my part of the deal?"

Roger put the $5,000 down on the table, atop the corpse. "Five grand. Each time I come in. No questions or any problems."

Whiskey's eyebrows jumped up. "Wow, so no negotiations or anything. I would've been okay with three grand, but I'll take five." Whiskey picked up the cash.

Roger smiled, relieved that he was so receptive to the proposal.

"Okay, so, now let's get to it. I'm *dead* serious. What do you need these parts for?"

Roger hesitated and became uneasy again. "I'd rather not say."

Whiskey curled his bottom lip and sat upright, taking another sip of his glass. "Okay, let me guess. I'm good at this." He sized Roger up. "You're a young guy. Don't strike me as a necrophiliac. Seem confident, so it's not anything with your overbearing parents. So . . . you lost a spouse or child recently."

Roger reacted ever so slightly to the word spouse, but Whiskey noticed it.

"And you have the body at home, don't you?" he asked rather inquisitively.

At this point Roger thought he should just come clean. "My wife." If anything happened, he could just deny it and the police would see how deranged and strange Mr. Whiskey was, clearing him of any blame.

"And you're not ready to say goodbye yet?" Whiskey nodded as if he understood Roger's predicament.

Roger stopped responding. He didn't want to share too much information with Whiskey. At least not at this point.

"Hey, RT, we don't have to get too personal if you don't like. As you can see"—he motioned to the bodies around him—"I don't have much company in my line of work. Herbie upstairs is the only person I speak with each day, and he's as useful as a dead body. But he pays me well and leaves me alone, so what the hell, right?" Whiskey jumped off the table and walked the cash to his desk in a small back area. "Okay, RT. Tell me what you need, and I'll cut the pieces off for you. Only thing is we keep this arrangement between us. Anything comes back to me, and I deny it."

Roger agreed.

"And I can only give you pieces of people that are to be cremated. No one will know that anything is missing. It could be a head for all they know. We just have to get them ashes.

But anyone I have to prep for a cemetery burial or viewing is off limits. And my skills are limited, so I won't be helping you dig up and/or retrieve anyone, as close as they may resemble your wife. This isn't going to be like *Weekend at Bernie's*, okay?"

Roger felt like Whiskey was too smooth and collected with everything, as if he'd done this sort of thing before.

Whiskey grabbed a very well-maintained electric bone saw and walked to the body of a woman nearby.

"What's today's order? Fingers? Piece of an abdomen? Pick your poison." Whiskey tensed up, his face eager with excitement.

Roger questioned whether Whiskey had done similar things to corpses prior. Maybe he enjoyed desecrating bodies?

"I need a set of toes," Roger responded hesitantly, still unsure what to make of his new ally.

"Toes. Whoa. I charge per toe, ya know," Whiskey said, smiling.

Roger shrugged.

"I'm just kidding, RT. We morticians have a weird sense of humor. Keeps us alive. Pun intended."

Mr. Whiskey is insane. But he's kind of fun to be around.

"Okay, five toes coming up, RT." Whiskey cut off the toes, placed them in a ziplock bag, and handed it to Roger.

Chapter 10

Camille awakened a day later at the top of the crypt again. It was later in the day, and the sun had already set. She rubbed her eyes, unsure how long she had been out. It took her a few minutes to figure out where she was, as her condition made her increasingly forgetful.

Oh, that hunger. That nasty, ugly hunger.

The only thing on her mind was the hunger. She crawled down from the crypt, and a cool breeze moved what was left of her hair. She felt her left eyelid twitch and she rubbed it, only to see it fall onto the ground. She was still able to see, but that side now had a wider lens, which threw off her perception.

Hungry...

She realized that there was no more food nearby, and if she wanted to keep herself put together, literally, she would need to leave the cemetery. She stumbled forward, catching her balance on the various-sized gravestones around her, and reached the gate near the street.

I smell it . . .

She fell forward but caught herself on her hands, feeling more comfortable walking on all fours. She trotted quickly toward the stench of a corpse. Camille made it several miles from the cemetery to the intersection of Orchard Lane and Valley View Drive.

I'm close . . . hungry . . . I recognize that smell. It's that woman. What was her name?

The skin started to peel off her hands from their continuous contact with the pavement. But the instincts drove her to the odor.

She continued up Orchard Lane, noticing none of the houses had any lights on and the street was almost as dark as the night sky. Camille slowly crawled house to house until she reached 723. She sniffed the sidewalk and was led to the side of Roger Todger's house.

* * *

Meanwhile, having just sewn the new toes onto Katie, Roger thought she looked amazing.

I miss you so much. I wish I could feel you with that life back in your body just once more.

He thought back to how sexual she was before her illness. And he hadn't been with her or done anything sexually in a long time.

He got an erection and began to rub the outside of his pants, feeling his growth.

You look so beautiful. Oh, Katie...

He pulled down his pants, watching his wife before him, imagining that she was just asleep. Not that he had ever pleasured himself to her while she rested, but the thought was getting near the actions of a necrophiliac and needed to be snuffed out so he could focus on the task at hand. Roger berated himself with self-degradation, knowing he was on the brink of an emotional collapse.

What are you doing?

This is disgusting! You should be ashamed of yourself.

Katie would hate you for this.

You're not strong enough to overcome her death.

You're weak, Roger!

He blocked out the negative thoughts, grunting loud, and took himself in his hand, beginning to pull. He remembered the silly way she would take her shirt off, whipping it across the room and giving him the cutest smile, every time they would be intimate. She was so incredibly sexy when she wanted to be. He imagined being with her again.

Katie, you feel so good.

He thought of making love to her and looking at her face, feeling connected to her in so many ways. Roger then thought of the last time she felt well enough to be intimate, which was more than a year ago. And she began her downhill slope to her eventual death. Roger would never feel her ever again.

She was one in a million. Ten million. You'll never find anyone else like her again.

He continued masturbating but increased the pace. A small amount of sweat bunched the skin of his shaft, rubbing to a blister, but he continued on. Perspiration dripped from his eyebrows, and he began to get dizzy.

Keep going, you piece of shit.

He scolded himself as a small wound opened up on the underside of his shaft and the pain now exceeded the pleasurable sensations. But he was determined to finish. He deserved this. He needed a release. And he needed this time with Katie.

"You wanna come in here and fuck some dead bodies, right?"

He scoffed at the thought of Whiskey's comment at the funeral home. He was not a necrophiliac. The mere thought disgusted him. This was his wife.

Shut up, Whiskey. I'm not touching her body. You're ruining this for me.

He continued and even yelped at the pain, looking down to see a small amount of blood all over himself, which did not stop him. He tensed his body to force himself to finish, which came later than he would have liked. He fell onto his backside, panting and completely fatigued. The entire experience felt good for a few brief seconds but made him feel awful beyond that.

What the fuck am I doing? First I play with dead bodies, now I'm jerking off to them?

Then he looked at Katie's face again. "I'm sorry. I shouldn't have done that," he said feeling remorseful.

He steadied himself to stand up but winced at the pain from a now openly bleeding cut on his penis.

"Oh shit," he said, rushing to the bathroom to clean himself up.

The relief he forced in such an unhealthy way created more problems than it solved.

As he moistened his dark purple washcloth with cold water, he dabbed at the cut, gently wiping the blood. He then washed his hands until they were raw and boiled them in the scalding water.

Wake up! You're losing it, Roger!

He splashed water on his face and looked up at himself in the mirror. His face looked like it had aged a decade in the last week. There were dark rings under his eyes, which were bloodshot, his face was unshaven, and he looked very unlike his normal well-put-together self.

Roger heard garbage pails fall over and ran to the window. Someone was outside his house, pulling the garbage bags apart. In a panic, he grabbed the metal doorstop and swung the side door wide open.

Oh no, someone knows what I've done. Maybe it's the police. They're going to try and take her from me.

"Hey, what the fuck are you doing out here!" he yelled at the person, not caring who or what they were.

Roger stopped at the sight of the thing, which was clearly eating something off the ground. He saw a partially bald head and dirty clothes atop a sickly-looking body crouched down on all fours. It slowly stopped chewing and raised its head to look at Roger, who was frozen in fear.

Camille had a partially missing eye and a long, split tongue hanging out of her mouth. The skin on her arms and face looked glued together like some sort of Frankenstein monster.

"Oh, Jesus Christ," he muttered as he noticed Katie's rotted toes that he had just thrown out an hour earlier.

It's eating the toes, for God's sake. Get in the house!

The abomination screeched at Roger, who retreated into the house. He locked the door and sat on the ground, out of sight, hearing the creature finish its meal and quietly leave.

Chapter 11

The following day, Roger walked into Mr. Whiskey's preparation room again.

"Yo, RT. Didn't think I'd see you back here so soon," he said in a very personable way, inviting Roger in.

"You didn't tell anyone about yesterday, right?" Roger was curious whether the monster at his house had some link to Whiskey.

Whiskey looked at him and laughed casually. "Hey, RT, I know you're *dying* to know something, so just ask me."

Roger wasn't particularly amused by all the euphemisms at that moment.

"It's strange. I had just sewed the new toes onto Katie—"

"Oh, that's her name. Katie . . ." Whiskey interrupted.

Roger ignored the interjection. "I put the old toes in the garbage, and they were very broken down and stank to high heaven."

"Yeah, decomposition sounds nicer than it really is. Stinky and mushy."

"But I caught some kind of... thing... eating the toes out of the garbage. Scared the hell out of me. I don't even know how to describe it to you."

Whiskey found his whiskey glass and sipped it again. "Yikes! Well, first off, I know that I look"—he waved his hands over his unimpressive body—"like I'm a super popular guy with the ladies and all. After all, morticians were tagging people long before Facebook, but sadly, no."

"Stop with the jokes for one goddamned minute!" Roger lost his patience.

"Okay, okay, okay. I see we've hit a bit of a *dead end* here, pal. So something freaky ate your dead wife's detached toes out of your garbage. I have that right?"

Roger nodded. "I just didn't know if you ever heard of something like that."

"Can't say that I have. At least not in real life. I'm a bit of a nerd, if you can believe that. Bodies and the supernatural fascinate me. So, if there's a show on finding bigfoot, the Loch Ness monster, that Blackheart thing from Meadowsville, or whatever else, I've seen it and know all about it." Whiskey shifted his head to a vast array of books on similar subjects near his desk.

"So what could it be?"

"Well, RT—"

"Look, RT sounds so dumb. Just call me Roger," Roger requested.

"Well, there we go. Our relationship just stepped forward," Whiskey said, smiling. "Unfortunately, I've never had anything cool about me besides the moniker 'Mr. Whiskey,' so I'm hanging on to that one, bud."

Roger loosened up a bit at Whiskey's humor and sat down on one of the metal tables. Whiskey's smooth delivery and quirky personality were enough to calm Roger a little.

"But, Roger, like ninety-five percent of cryptids and potential monsters supposedly eat body parts. So I'd need a little more information before I could determine what the hell that thing could be. It obviously found you and likes how your wife tastes, so this could be the closest you ever get to a sort of ménage à trois, huh?" Whisky leaned in, showing more teeth than a baboon.

Roger laughed a little. "You're one fucked up person, Whiskey. You know that?"

"Roger, I work a job where I'm on call twenty-four-seven with no one to cover. Don't have the time for friendships or relationships. And even if I did, this sort of profession isn't something the ladies look for. Even if I used a pickup line on them like, 'Hey, baby, you look good. Like open casket good.' They're just not into it. And even if I were married and had kids, you think this profession allows for a bring-your-kids-to-work day or anything? Needless to say, if I can make even one person smile, and not because I'd stitched their face to look like that, I'd say that I'm doing something good."

Roger listened to his logic and nodded, understanding it.

"Now, Roger, do me a favor. You look like shit. Go get some rest. Hell, if you wanna borrow my hearse and have some fun, go order a Happy Meal in it. Watch the confused looks you get."

Roger laughed again. He hadn't laughed this much in a while but enjoyed it.

"Thanks, Whiskey. I'll be back soon." He started to make his way out of the area.

"Hey, Roger," Whiskey yelled, taking a small bottle of Jim Beam out from under one of the preparation tables. "If you see that thing again, try to get a picture or watch it for a bit. Get some more intel, and we'll try to pin down what it is. But don't go searching for it. Could be dangerous."

Roger nodded and left. He went home and didn't go clean up his mess down by Katie. His cleaning habits had been interrupted by the deluge of exhaustion. He fell into bed and slept for nine straight hours.

Chapter 12

Roger woke up to the sound of his house phone but couldn't move to pick it up. The answering machine responded.

"Hey, this is Roger."
"And Katie," she said.
"Please leave a message, and we'll get back to you soon," they said together.

Roger smiled at the sound of her voice.

"Hey, bubbie, it's Mom. Haven't heard from you since we got back and just wanted to check in. Dad and I love you so much and are here if you need anything. If you can get some time off work, try to fly out and stay with us for a little while. Might be nice to get away from the house. But call when you have a chance."

He'd been so focused on preserving Katie that he hadn't responded to any of the messages people had been leaving for him. But they'd understand. He was busy right now.

Roger sat up and saw the alarm clock sitting at six o'clock. No wonder he was an early riser—his parents raised him that way. He got up and looked at his cellphone. There was one missed call and a voicemail. He hit the button and heard a familiar voice.

"Hey, Roger . . . it's Allison Miller. From . . . well, hopefully you remember. Just wanted to call and check in. Again, I was really sorry to hear about Katie but enjoyed our chat at the funeral. Gosh, that still sounds so strange to say out loud. But if you want, give me a call. I'd love to hear from you. Bye!"

The message was from yesterday. Between work and everything else, he hadn't even cleaned the house or checked his phone until now.

I gotta find a balance with everything. And it's too soon to talk to another woman like that. It's not right.

He battled his thoughts, unsure whether to ever have another relationship or brave the rest of his life alone.

What would Katie want me to do?

As he stood, every part of his body ached. He hadn't slept like that in a long time. His education taught him when a person reduced the effects of their sympathetic nervous system, letting their body finally relax after chronic stress, it finally recuperated a bit. And it could leave them sore and fatigued initially.

He did a few minutes of gentle stretching to limber up and went to the basement to check on Katie. The smell was getting worse each day, and her body was rapidly declining. He'd have to go see Whiskey again soon.

He turned to leave the room and stepped on the mess he made last night, feeling the congealed puddle squish under his toes.

"I can see this is going to be the start of a good day," he said to himself sarcastically.

He took off his shirt and cleaned the ejaculate off his foot, looking down at Katie. Surprisingly, her face was holding up well, but her chest was now sinking in, her hands rotting, and that strange bite mark on her thigh seemed to be breaking down quicker than anything else.

He thought of that creature again. It didn't attack, so he doubted how dangerous it could be. But it now knew where he lived. And he needed to be careful until he knew more about it.

* * *

As Roger got ready for work and left his house, he didn't realize Camille was lying in one of his neighbor's wooden sheds in their backyard.

She was much too weak to get back to the cemetery right now. She needed to feed more to be able to make that journey. But she had already tasted Katie several times now and wanted more.

I'm ... so ... hungry. Need body ... She lost more of herself as the hunger persisted.

Chapter 13

Roger came home that night exhausted from a long service report meeting between himself, his operations manager, and site contact. The contact, Alex, had his job because his uncle was on the board of directors for Tick Tech Logistics. But beyond that, he had no knowledge of computer parts or how to manage a worksite. So Alex focused most of his critiques on the coaching program on what he felt the employees needed rather than the detailed reporting that indicated otherwise. Roger's manager explained how he developed an annual service plan, but Alex stayed strong in his stance. He wanted it his way and didn't want to hear another word about it. As much as Tom wanted to help, he had to yield to the demands of the site contact. Roger kept quiet and swallowed his frustrations.

The house looked like a mess. Clothes were all over. Everything was dusty. And he had nervous energy from today. Roger started pulling out all of his mandatory cleaning supplies, including his fuzzy duster, furniture polish, vinegar surface cleaner, and diluted bleach. He spent the next four hours scrubbing every inch of the house, getting it to his extremely high standards. It felt good to be active again and not feel disgusted when he looked around his own home.

The last room he needed to clean was where Katie was lying. He put everything down and brought a broom into the storage area. Her hands were almost hanging off, with some very weak soft tissue holding on by threads. The blackened deterioration smelled like rotted meat, making Roger gag.

She can't stay here much longer. You can't keep this up.

Roger carefully took his utility knife and cut off both the hands, putting them in two separate plastic bags. He then took off the section of her thigh where the bite mark was, storing it the same way as the hands.

There's almost nothing left of her. You have to say goodbye at some point.

Roger brought the bags upstairs and put them outside the side door again, hoping to get another glimpse of the monster. He was both curious and frightened by its presence.

* * *

Camille awoke. She smelled the rotted flesh immediately when the owner brought it outside and perked up inside the wooden shed. As she managed to sloppily find her footing, she knocked over a few small planting pots and rattled some rakes hanging off hooks. She couldn't put a word together in her mind and had now devolved into something completely unworldly. But she was still inside . . . somewhere.

A small squeak made her look down. Several baby mice were cuddled together among a tiny patch of leaves. A guttural rumble escaped her lungs, and she lowered herself down, nose to nose with the defenseless creatures. But the hunger grew, and the mice were too small to bring her any form of satiety. The stench of the body she had previously feasted on was strong. And it was waiting for her. It managed to enter the dilapidated woodshed through every hole and crack. Like invisible smoke. It enveloped her body and brought about every aspect of her ghoulish appearance in its most primal form. The hunger was all that mattered now. She pushed through the hinged door with her forehead, looking into the night, across at the man she previously encountered.

* * *

Roger continued to open the bags and squeeze the air out, trying to get the smell into the night. He realized he didn't have any weapons so kept the door ajar in case he needed to run back inside again.

What makes you think it can't go inside?

He shook the thought and noticed something in the dark across the street. It walked on all fours but had humanlike features, mostly female, despite sections of its exposed body not matching the others. The body looked larger than he remembered, and the clothes it had worn were now torn all over, barely hanging on or covering anything up.

Roger set down his wife's hands and stepped back, watching the monster creep forward, sniffing the ground like a dog tracing a scent.

It looked up with pained eyes, and he felt sorry for whatever it was. Living in the dark and eating body parts could not be a pleasant lifestyle.

"It's okay. I'm not going to hurt you," he said, crouching down.

Camille began licking the skin off the hands with her rough, catlike tongue. She placed her disfigured hands on either side of the meat, now chewing through the bone slowly.

Roger wished he could get a picture for Whiskey but didn't want to scare it off. He just watched it eat, forgetting that it was Katie's hands being devoured. He wanted to know what this creature was. And why it wanted Katie's parts so badly.

The creature finished the hands but then turned to the piece of thigh meat. It smelled the chunk of meat and reared its head back, pausing briefly at the bite mark. Roger noticed the hesitation and deduced that this thing created it.

"It was you," he said softly.

The creature flared its drooping nostrils at Roger. It then quickly ate the thigh portion and started shaking briefly.

* * *

Camille looked down at her hands, and the skin regrew and shifted into human features. She then looked down at her leg and saw that the portion of Katie's thigh now matched hers too.

The man's jaw dropped as the changes happened.

Who is this person? Camille regained some semblance of awareness after the feeding. *Why is he feeding me? Why do I want it?*

"Oh wow," he said to Camille. "So you have to eat, or you fall apart. And the pieces become you."

Camille, starting to feel more of her logic and strength return, understood some of what he said, but she still couldn't find much control over her body. Something else inside was overpowering her and limiting her abilities.

"Yaaa . . ." she screeched, before running off on two legs to preserve her new hands.

* * *

"Wow," Roger said, staying in his position. He had no idea what he just witnessed but wanted to know more about it. And he had to tell Whiskey about his findings at some point.

Chapter 14

Roger stood in the grocery store staring at the meat selections. Suddenly, all of the products had more meaning. He picked up a package of pork chops and imagined a pig dancing with its body diagrammed for the ribs, bacon, chops, and all the delicious parts of the animal. He smiled to himself, unaware of his further plunge into insanity.

He put the chops down and picked up a large chuck roast. There was a little blood underneath the shrink wrap that coated his hand. He thought of the fluid on him as he tried to sew Katie's new hands onto her body. It had a little bit of blood but resembled some sort of uncongealed green gelatin. Whatever was injected into her body to keep it preserved.

"Fuckin' Jell-O," he muttered to himself.

"Excuse me?" an older woman, wearing an absolutely hideous sweater with a German shepherd's face on it, asked him.

Roger had been so entranced by the meat section that he didn't realize anyone else was around.

"Oh, sorry. Nothing," he said, putting the roast back and grabbing a few packs of boneless chicken breasts.

"Your hand," she responded, looking at the blood. "Are you injured?"

Roger didn't feel much in the mood for talking to anyone now and couldn't even find the energy to muster up an insincere response.

"You know the old expression. Where there's blood, there's meat, right?" he said, hoping to scare her off.

The woman shook her head in disgust and walked away.

"I'd be angry if I dressed like that too," he muttered, uncaring if she heard.

Roger left the meat section and began walking quickly through the store. Aside from getting the bare essentials, he was focused on getting to see Whiskey in a few hours and trying to get Katie new hands. The first attempt at repairs was not good—her skin was breaking down more each day, making it less able to be manipulated.

But that creature he'd now encountered twice was something else. Really something that he wanted to understand better.

It's a bad idea, what you're thinking, Roger. And you know it.

Oh, shut up in there. I'm not going to feed my wife's body to that thing just so it will look like her. I'm not that far gone.

"God help my sanity, I've even begun fighting with myself now," he said, walking quickly to the dairy section.

Roger finished at the store and drove home. At his front door was an edible arrangement. He quickly looked at the tag that read *Hope you're holding up, Roger. We're here if you need anything. Love, Ken and Darla.* Roger rolled his eyes at the kind gesture from Katie's friends but then quickly thought of the negatives.

Of course this comes right after I go shopping. This is too much fruit for just me. What were they thinking? Just going to rot and be thrown away. Like Katie.

He stomped the edible arrangement and tossed it into the garbage pail outside. He then placed all the groceries in their respective spots in the kitchen. He checked the time; it was six twenty-five, so he needed to wait until tonight's event at the funeral home was completed before he could go see Whiskey.

His house was still spotless from his cleaning frenzy. What used to be a daily obsessive-compulsive routine was now totally different since he was all alone. He looked at the handwritten list on the dry-erase board in the kitchen near the side door. It appeared Katie rewrote it at some point, unbeknownst to him, because it was now legible and elegant. His penmanship looked much like a cross between a doctor and a first grader. On the plus side, as he jotted down his interaction notes at work, even if he lost his paperwork, no one would be able to decipher the script.

Monday: Wipe windows
Tuesday: Polish furniture

Wednesday: Dust
Thursday: Mop and deep vacuum
Friday: Bathrooms
Saturday: Kitchen
Sunday: Roger, take a break!

It all has to change. All of it.

He stopped for a minute and thought of a time a few years ago when she toyed with him like that. She always loved giving him a playful hard time on his cleaning habits.

"Roger, you missed a spot."
"No, I didn't," he said, not sure if it was a joke or not. "Wait—where?" He looked around the room.
"Here," she yelled and lifted her foot, laughing.
Roger smiled and grabbed her leg, kissing the top of her foot.

He attributed his cleanliness to his mother, who was the type of person who didn't like to see dust or even a few drops of water in the kitchen sink. She turned cleaning into an Olympic event, and Roger inherited that work ethic. But Katie appreciated his hard work, especially when she became so sick. She would spend days on the couch, just buried under a blanket, unable to talk much or move around. He took care of everything for her. And he would sit on her preferred cushy armchair across from her most nights, just watching her.

Too sick to even enjoy her favorite chair. This isn't fair.

Even if he couldn't see her, he wanted to be there in case she needed anything. He was just a prisoner, watching her wither away with nothing he could do. Just like now.

But he smiled at the memory and continued onward to the storage area of the basement. He checked on Katie several times a day, but today the smell was worse than ever. Her body was shifted to the right side a bit now and had developed a deeper greenish hue. The toes he reattached had fallen off too. The thigh area was somehow still secure. He formed a conclusion but didn't want to admit it to himself.

She can't stay here. You should probably ask Whiskey to rent space in one of his freezers and continue to pay him whatever he asks.

Yeah, I'm sure that's why Katie left you all that life insurance money. So you could not pay bills and use it to keep her body intact because you're too weak to deal with it and move on.

"Oh, shut up!" he yelled to himself, conflicted on what to do. "I know I can get over this. And I will. I'm just not ready yet."

He fumed with his internal dialogue as another one of Katie's toes fell off, barely held on by the black thread he used. Her lips had also begun sagging to the right side.

"I need whiskey. Both kinds." He sighed, thinking of Mr. Whiskey and a glass of it to calm his nerves.

He quickly ran upstairs and drove over to see Whiskey.

* * *

As he got out of the car, he saw a funeral already underway.

I need this.

Feeling emotionally distraught and needy, he walked in, still dressed in his work clothes. The bulk of the attendees were much older than him, which he imagined was the case in most instances. Roger walked in while the priest was speaking up front to a group of maybe fifty people. He grabbed a seat in back and paused, appreciating being around other people. Unlike work, these people didn't want anything from him. They didn't want to talk at him or request anything of him. As far as they were concerned, he was here as a member of their group of the forlorn.

The few bodies he had seen from Whiskey all looked amazingly good.

You sure you don't want him working on Katie? You'd rather her waste away for a second time?

"Shush!" he said to himself, drawing several wrinkled faces looking back at him.

Emotional now, between strife and anxiety, he had to decide what to do about his wife's body. He was angry with himself because he couldn't properly process Katie passing. Being in his midthirties, he had never lost anyone close to him. It was a hard learning curve.

Pull yourself together.

A few lone tears fell down his face, and he acted like his previous sound had been a sniffle, which was believable. Everyone turned away from him again.

An older man sitting next to him forcefully grabbed his hand and nodded at him. He didn't owe Roger anything and could have just ignored him as a perfect stranger. But he saw Roger's sadness and offered him a helping hand. Just to be nice. Roger responded with a slight grip and they both sat, watching the ceremony wrap up over the next few minutes.

Roger focused on breathing and calming his body.

You'll figure this out. Stay strong.

He heard the words in his own mind and smiled, closing his eyes.

You drive me nuts, brain, but I always appreciate the input.

The ceremony ended and everyone started to leave. There were fewer sad and crying faces here than with other funerals he'd been to. He wondered whether it was because as one got older, they were just waiting to die. It sounded morbid, but it was more likely the older a person got. So it wasn't much of a surprise or shock when it happened to those around them either.

Before going downstairs to see Mr. Whiskey, he made sure to shake hands with and thank the kind gentleman who comforted him. He stopped at the doorway, hearing Whiskey singing to himself.

"I see the sun come up and take a drink. Then I go to bed with Jack Daniels every night."

Roger knocked and there was no answer. He slowly opened the door and saw Whiskey working on someone's face. He smiled at how nonchalantly Whiskey was working on a dead body. He then saw his signature sipping glass of whiskey nearby.

He is out of his mind.

"Whiskey," Roger said out loud, but Whiskey didn't hear him.

"Wake up and do it all over again. Whiskey is my lifeblood!" he sang out loud now, spinning his chair.

He saw Roger and fell off, holding his heart and panting. Roger noticed his T-shirt, which had a stick figure lying on the ground and read *Casual-tee*.

"Holy Christ on a cracker, Roger. You almost . . . well . . . turned me into one of these guys," he said, pointing around to the bodies. "Well, don't keep me in suspense. What can I do ya for?" He straightened himself out. "How's the little lady doing?"

Roger tensed at the question. "Well, not great, if you must know."

Whiskey put up his hands. "Let me guess. Your little idea of sewing other people's parts to her isn't panning out, right?"

Roger nodded, looking at the ground. "Listen, I was thinking. I can pay you more." He took another wad of cash out of his pocket.

"Jesus, what do you do for a living?" Whiskey laughed. "I'm *dead* serious. Where do you keep getting all that money?"

"Katie's life insurance."

Whiskey raised an eyebrow and smirked. "But I'm sure she had other ideas as to how you'd spend it. Like mortgage. Food. Stuff like that?"

Roger shrugged. "I'm not ready to say goodbye yet, Whiskey," he admitted.

Whiskey gave Roger an empathic look. "I get it. Well, tell you what. It's been a little slow around here, so I have a few minutes to chat." Whiskey pulled up a rusted steel folding chair.

"Now, I'd offer you a drink. But as you can see, the only cold ones around here are the ones with faces. Am I right?" Whiskey said, slapping Roger on the arm.

Roger looked up and tried not to laugh. "Whiskey, you should be a comedian if this mortician business doesn't work out. I really think you have something."

"Maybe. But I'm too good. And I love my work." He pushed the slicked hair off his forehead. "So let's talk about your little problem."

"Can you work on her for me? Do all the work and keep her together for as long as possible?"

Roger felt like he let his wife down. He couldn't keep her intact, but he'd grown to trust Whiskey. He was the best person for the job now.

"Yeah, sure can. I always have some empty space in the freezers," Whiskey stated. "Only thing is, she goes to the bottom of the priority list, my man. Just the way it is. Herbie up there leaves me alone as long as I keep the production line going. You get it."

Roger nodded. "Understood."

"But, Rog, I'll be honest. We're going on almost two weeks. She's not going to last much longer. So I'll do my best, but no promises," he said rather seriously.

"Do what you can. I know that I'll have to let her go. It's just not the right time," Roger responded, looking down as his eyes welled up.

Whiskey awkwardly extended a hand to put on his shoulder. "Hey, Roger. Cheer up. I know this isn't fun to think about. But one day you'll be laughing about this. How many people can say that they stole their wife's corpse, tried to sew it up with other people's body parts, and bribed a smart-mouthed mortician? You're one in a million. No, ten million."

Just like Katie. We were meant to be.

Roger smiled. "Just wish I could've done more for her." A tear fell down his left cheek.

"I get it. Hey, I have a closed casket funeral tomorrow. I was gonna ask Herbie upstairs to play 'Pop Goes the Weasel' at the very end. You should swing by and watch the reactions. Priceless!"

Roger didn't smile or laugh.

"I promise to be as gentle and accurate as I can with Katie. No worries there." Whiskey patted Roger on the knee.

Roger got up and started to leave. "I'll pack her up and bring her over tomorrow. She's in bad shape, so I hope you're as good as you say you are."

Whiskey looked surprised at the comment. "You see the people I put on display up there." He pointed up toward the viewing rooms. "They're immaculate."

Roger opened the door, but Whiskey yelled to him. "You see that thing by your house again? Any new info there?"

Roger shut the door, almost forgetting about the creature due to his internal conflicts. "Actually, I did, and you're going to have a field day with this one. I'm *dead* serious." He forced himself to finally join in the fun with Whiskey's constant references.

"There we go! I know you could do it." Whiskey tossed a fist up to the ceiling in celebration. "Death doesn't have to be tragic. It's inevitable, so we might as well have some fun with it."

They sat, and Roger explained everything he saw the previous day with the monstrosity.

Chapter 15

Back at Roger's house, Camille returned, despite the lack of smelling anything fresh. She spent the last day remembering more about herself and being able to walk upright again. She'd quickly figured out that the more she fed, the more control she had over herself. She was also able to maneuver all the way to and from the graveyard but wasn't sure what kept calling her back there.

The houses around 723 Orchard Lane all had their porch lights on, so she was careful not to raise any suspicion. She opened the garbage pail lid, admiring her pretty new hands, and pulled the bag open. There were no appetizing odors. Just some squished fruit and ribbons.

"Argh!" she grunted, shoving the pail over.

I need to keep eating if I hope to keep my mind and body intact.

Then the sweet odor of Katie's body seeped out of a cracked window in the upstairs of the house.

"Inside. Get inside," she grumbled.

She grabbed ahold of the tan siding of the house and crawled up toward the window like a large spider. She was still in a state of disarray, and she was unaware, until that moment, of her ability to climb like that. But whatever she was battling with for control of her body was stronger and had increased abilities.

Camille opened the window and slipped inside the master bedroom. She looked around and saw a queen bed, two matching side lights, and armoires. The entire room was spotless and totally symmetrical, lined with several pictures of Katie and Roger. They seemed so happy together. She had some flashbacks of her apartment in Meadowsville. It was the same exact setup but with only one of everything. She wished there were someone else with her in that apartment, but she hadn't been lucky enough to be in a significant relationship for quite some time. It made her reminisce of home.

I wish I had someone like this guy. To accept and love me for what I was. What I am.

"Home..." she said, feeling at ease here, smelling the odor again.

She shimmied forward on still uneven legs and got to the plain hallway leading down the stairs to the front foyer. She heard the night breeze whistle through another room and looked to see a smaller, empty bedroom with a lightly used crib in it, covered in dust.

Camille slunk down the steps and looked around the living room and hallway leading to the kitchen. She walked forward, using the walls as support, and reached the basement door. She smelled the rotting decay of Katie's increasingly frail body. She pulled the door hard, almost off the hinges, and stumbled down the carpeted basement stairs, eager for another meal. The basement had a speckled gray epoxy paint floor and all-white walls. Camille's bare foot slammed down with a softened slap. The smell was overpowering now. Her logic slipped away.

Please don't go! Get control back!

Her ambitions were of no use. The monster was taking over again. She lurched toward the large wooden door leading to the storage area. The door stuck a tiny bit, but she powered it open, and a storm of stink assaulted her olfactory sense. Katie lay on an acrylic blanket on the cement floor. The body was greenish, with various parts hanging off and clearly nearing complete decomposition. Camille crouched down and took in the sight. The first complete body she'd been near in some time now.

Her long, gnarled black tongue emerged from her lips and began licking Katie's collar area. The skin absorbed into the wet sandpaper-like protuberance like cooked oatmeal. Camille continued licking the skin off like a hungry animal. She then continued with the left shoulder before she heard a noise from upstairs. She froze, unsure of what to do.

It's him. He can't see me here.

* * *

Roger readied to pack Katie up and take her over to Whiskey the next day. Whiskey had advised Roger to be extremely careful, as any slipups could result in a catastrophic impact to the corpse. Whiskey also recommended that Roger wrap the entire body in plastic wrap.

He grabbed several rolls out of the drawer in the kitchen, turning to go to the basement, when he noticed a few smudges on the freshly mopped hardwood floor. He put the plastic wrap down on the counter and saw the basement door open.

It's in the house, Roger. Get out of the house!

He ignored his intuition and went downstairs quietly, only to see Camille feasting on Katie. He felt his heart drop.

"No, please stop. Stop that!" he yelled.

Camille turned around, now fully visible in the light. Roger saw not only Katie's hands as part of the creature but also now parts of her neck, chest, and arms. He put his hands to his mouth in horror and stepped forward. He was absolutely furious but didn't want to put himself in further danger, so he thought back to some of his old training on de-escalation techniques.

"It's okay," he said softly, stepping back, watching Camille lick her fading lips. "I just want to know what you are."

Camille, getting more nourishment, was better able to verbalize herself. But she could not say the words as well as she could think them.

I'm in here. Please help me!

"Cam-eel," the creature forced out. "I . . . Cam-eel."

"Camille?" Roger asked, hoping he was accurate as he felt the sweat on his back pull his shirt against his body.

Camille shook her head around like a dog trying to dry off.

"Camille, that's my wife, Katie. You can't have her, I'm afraid," he reasoned. "She belongs here with me."

Threatened, Camille snarled. In her mind, she understood what he was saying and felt sorry for what she had done to Katie, but her body was reacting badly to Roger's plea.

"No, no, it's okay. I'm not going to hurt you. What are you doing here?" he asked.

"Cam-eel... need... food..." she responded, swaying a bit.

Roger swallowed hard. "I can get you food. You eat people?" he asked, thinking of Whiskey's nonstop inventory of corpses.

"Cam-eel... need food... now!" she yelled, turning back around to Katie, biting her thigh, taking a big chunk out and chewing on it.

"Camille, please stop. You can't have her," he pleaded.

Camille had enough sense to feel empathy for him and his deceased wife. *I'm so sorry. Please help me. Give me more food and maybe I'll be able to speak to you. I just need this hunger to go away so I can focus.*

She screeched, barreling through him, and ran through the house, breaking out the front door.

Roger collected himself and took off after her. He again was thankful at this time to be in such good shape.

Camille ran through the streets, and Roger followed several hundred feet behind. He tried to pace himself, feeling the burning in his legs and chest, but overrode his sensory input and continued on. He took full breaths and tried to bring in as much fresh oxygen as possible. They ended up at the gates of the Holy Name Catholic Church cemetery.

Roger leaned over, resting his hands on his knees, catching his breath and watching Camille climb a crypt a little way in, putting herself just out of sight. He wondered whether to go home or proceed in.

He heard something call his name from behind.

Father Clark walking a small white poodle. "Roger, is that you?"

Just what I need right now.

"Roger Todger, I gave up hope to ever see you again. What brings you here?"

Roger, staring at the priest, was dripping with sweat and totally fatigued.

"Just . . . out for . . . a run," he replied.

"Well, that's great. Always a great tool to keep ourselves healthy, right?" He giggled. "We must preserve the blessings God gave us."

Roger saw no humor in the statement and had no time or patience for this person. He felt his nice-guy streak running out quickly.

"Did you give any more thought to my invitation? We'd love to have you as a member here. Plenty to do and lots of opportunities for a person like yourself. And there are plenty of eligible ladies your age in my congregation too."

Is this guy kidding me?

Roger's anger spiraled out of control. "Listen, Clark . . . I'm not close with God. I may be one day but not right now. And

I don't need some overly enthusiastic, self-proclaimed servant of God acting as a middleman for my conversation with Him. I'll talk to Him myself, when I'm goddamned good and ready. Now finish walking that cotton ball with eyes and leave me the fuck alone." He stared the poodle down, making it whimper.

Father Clark took a breath and stood upright, dejected. "Well, I'm sorry you feel that way. Have a good night, Mr. Todger. My thoughts are still with you." He quickly walked away.

Roger was happy to see him go and turned back to the graveyard.

He walked in and toward the large, pristine crypt. "Camille, I'm sorry I scared you before. I just want to talk."

Camille stayed hidden on the top of the structure. *I want to talk too. I can't control myself much anymore, but I'm here!*

"My name is Roger. Rodger Todger."

She stifled a snicker and then moved around a little.

Great, even monsters laugh at my shitty name, he thought.

Camille's gnarled face peered over the edge, down toward him. Some drool escaped her mouth, and it plopped down beside him.

"Camille, I'd like to know more about you. Is that okay?"

She completed an awkward nod of her head.

"Where do you come from?"

Camille tried to put the words together clearly, but it was so hard when malnourished and with parts of her face falling off.

Something happened in Meadowsville, and I ended up like this!

"Mead . . . ow . . . ville."

Roger couldn't believe she survived whatever actually happened in Meadowsville. Almost everyone had been killed, from what he had heard. One of the biggest disasters in American history.

"Were you once human?"

She moved her head again. Roger then noticed that the body she was wearing was more like a costume and there was something else living beneath it, moving slightly independently of her other parts.

"How did you become like this?" He motioned to her body.

"Don't . . . know . . ."

"And you eat people to stay alive?" he asked.

I don't want to. This monster inside me makes me do it.

"Cam-eel need food. Keep . . . body . . . same," she said.

Roger understood. She was a victim of the attack on Meadowsville and somehow was plagued with this condition where she needed to eat human flesh to stay alive. He wanted to help her, especially because she had parts of Katie's flesh on her body. He needed to ask Whiskey for more bodies—and fast.

"I can help you, Camille." Roger slipped into his work persona a bit. "Would you be okay with that?"

Yes! Thank you, Roger!

She grunted as Roger looked at Katie's neck forming under the monstrous face of Camille. She quickly went back into hiding, and Roger left the cemetery, knowing full well what he must do.

Chapter 16

Roger stood at work speaking with another employee about their health.

I wonder what she is. Is she a demon?

He pondered Camille's situation.

She clearly doesn't have anyone to help her. And now that I have Mr. Whiskey as an ally, I'm sure I can get her a consistent supply of body parts. And she can be okay. Right?

"Roger?" the division manager, Eric, said, with no response from Roger. "Hey, Roger! Earth to Roger!"

Roger snapped out of his thoughts and realized he completely missed the entire dialogue from Eric. He felt foolish—he'd never been this inattentive at work.

"I apologize. Not sure where my mind just went," he said, trying his best to remember the beginning of their conversation but failing miserably. He decided to make a general reflection statement to elicit something he could work with. "So let's weigh the pros and cons of that idea, shall we?"

Eric looked at him, confused. "Well, I could either get the colonoscopy or go against my doctor's recommendation and cancel it."

Fuck!

Humiliated, Roger tried to deflect. "So going with your gastroenterologist's recommendations will always be the best idea, of course." He again tried to make the conversation work and save himself from being even more embarrassed. "But I'm feeling that you still seem a bit trepidatious?" *Fingers crossed.*

"Well, sort of," Eric replied. "This would be my first time, and I've heard the prep for it is awful. You gotta drink that solution and shit your brains out for a full day before, right?"

BINGO!

"Yeah, the preparation is definitely the most uncomfortable and difficult part of the process. But it's a necessary evil, as the doctor needs to see a clear view of your bowel so he can accurately diagnose any issues there."

Eric continued listening. "Is there any way to make it easier?"

Roger shook his head, acting deep in thought. "It's tricky. I'd say if you can stay home the day before, definitely opt for that. And set up a little area near the bathroom to stay most of the day. Just try to rest and binge a TV show or some movies. You won't feel like doing much else, so anticipate a quiet day home. And also keep plenty of toilet paper, Vaseline, and such handy too."

Eric nodded, understanding only so much could be done. "So when is the procedure?"

"Four days from now." Eric became quiet and looked down at his keyboard for a few seconds. "I'm just afraid they may find something in there."

Roger leaned on the chair in front of him, as he was standing while Eric sat at his desk. He sensed fear in Eric's voice, a feeling Roger knew all too well.

"I'll always be honest with you, Eric." Roger softened his voice. "There is always that chance. But statistically, it's a ninety to ninety-five percent chance nothing is found, and even if there is a polyp, it can be removed and it's a done deal."

Eric smiled at the odds in his favor.

"You don't have any family history of anything. You have no symptoms that warrant concern. And you're just fifty years old. So, again, the chances of an issue are very low. But if there is anything there, you'll be catching it so early, it can be resolved easily, and you'll be in the clear."

Eric breathed a sigh of relief.

"It's not a walk in the park. But I really admire how proactive you're being with your health. And I'll be here to help you through it. I'll have my phone on twenty-four-seven, as usual, so please feel free to call me anytime during all this if you have any other questions. We'll get you through it. Promise."

Eric nodded and smiled wider. "Thank you for all that, Roger. We can always count on you. All of us here." Eric stood up and shook Roger's hand.

They parted, and Roger immediately remembered going home last night and shrink-wrapping his wife's body in preparation for Whiskey to take over. When he rolled Katie over, the smell was worse than he could imagine, and there was a puddle of embalming fluid and loose tissue under her, partially absorbed by the blanket. He gagged at the sight and smell but continued on. Now he would just have to wait until nightfall so he could put Katie in his car and drive her to the funeral home.

On his ride home, he noticed another call from Allison Miller.

I really should respond. I don't want to be rude. She's just being nice, is all.

He still felt like it would be disrespectful to Katie, but he texted Allison a quick message: Hi, Allison! Great to hear from you. Sorry I've been off the grid. Work has been really hectic. We'll catch up soon. Hope you're well!

Roger wasn't in the mindset right now to even entertain the idea of having friends or, in Allison's case, maybe something more. There was just too much happening right now.

You'll have to move on eventually.

"I know, I know," he said, acknowledging the inevitable.

After he got home, he waited until the sun set around seven o'clock to try and move her into the car. Her body was not in a good state at this point, and aside from her bones keeping the basic structure, everything else was moving around and liquid-y. It was like moving a dense waterbed. He struggled to pull her up the stairs but eventually made it. At this point, he was less concerned about the damage he did to the body and totally focused on his wife. He continued pulling at the plastic wrap, getting the body out into his single-car garage and into the back seat of the vehicle. Between the pursuit with Camille last night and now this, his body needed a rest. The soreness in his thighs and shoulders was tremendously uncomfortable.

Roger sat in the driver's seat and caught his breath. He hoped he wasn't pulled over by a cop en route to the funeral home. The ride was only about fifteen minutes and hopefully would go smoothly.

When he arrived, Mr. Whiskey waited outside by himself. As soon as Roger opened the door, his friend stood to attention, wearing a shirt that read *Eat, sleep, embalm, repeat.*

"So I finally get to meet the little lady," Whiskey said sarcastically. "I have a small lift in the back that we can lower her down to my work area. Help me move her."

Both men took opposite ends of the body and got it to the downstairs of the funeral home.

Whiskey placed her on a wheeled metal table and began to peel the covering off. "Now, Roger, judging by the time she died and how this body feels, I really can't guarantee much at all."

Roger took another bundle of hundred dollar bills out of his pants pocket and slapped it down on the table.

Whiskey raised an eyebrow and looked at it in wonder. "You're getting good at that. And I'll do my best with her. I know this is quite different from other cases that I've worked on. Quite a bit of a challenge. I'll put some time in. Give me until tomorrow, and you can come by and I'll update you," Whiskey said, starting to cut the wrap off Katie, working carefully not to damage the body.

Roger and Whiskey looked at Katie's corpse in silence, both in admiration.

"Roger, she really was beautiful. I'm not kidding around. I'm so sorry you lost her like this."

Roger's eyes became glassy and he nodded, looking at his wife. Even with the body decomposing, her beauty shone through.

Whiskey turned into his professional self. Roger had not seen this side of him yet but was fairly impressed.

Whiskey put on plastic gloves and examined Katie's face more closely. "Let's see here. Little wax reconstruction for the face." He moved her eyelids and mouth around. "Maybe some cotton to build up the cheeks and mouth again. I can't do any tricks with the circulatory system at this point." Whiskey leaned away from Katie and looked seriously at Roger. "Hey, Roger, I gotta ask you something." He paused for a second before looking up. "What's the end game here?"

Roger turned his head, unsure of the agenda at hand.

"No, I'm not trying to pick on you or anything. I'll work on her and make her look like new again. But it won't last. She's already been gone about two weeks, which is the limit for a preserved body like this. And I won't be able to keep working on her much longer before it all just disintegrates and falls apart."

Roger put his hands up to interrupt. "Whiskey, I get it." He looked down at the floor and fought back tears. "I'm . . ."

"I know. I've heard you say it a bunch. You're just not ready to say goodbye. But buddy, the clock is ticking. It will happen. And we can only do so much here. You have to be ready for that moment. It'll be over and she'll be gone. But you have to be prepared to keep living. She'd want you to."

Roger teared up at the brutal reality check. "Thanks, Whiskey. I know." He stood up and looked around the room, noticing a new addition to Whiskey's book collection: *Ghouls, Goblins, and Ghosts: The Definitive Guide to Creatures That Haunt Your Dreams.*

He really is into this stuff, isn't he?

"Whiskey, there's one other thing," Roger said hesitantly. "I need another favor."

"What's that?"

"I need body parts."

Whiskey looked confused. "But Katie is here."

"They're not for Katie."

Chapter 17

Roger sat in the cemetery with a plastic bag full of pieces from a random corpse that Whiskey gave him access to. He was careful not to take anything from the chest, shoulders, thighs, hands, or feet, as those parts of Camille already reflected Katie and would be affected.

He resisted the urge to whistle to avoid offending Camille. He anticipated her smelling the meat and coming out of hiding.

No more than two minutes later, Camille emerged from atop the crypt where he previously spoke to her. She was back on all fours and moved toward him, crawling down the side with ease.

God, what is this thing?

Heart heavy, he watched Katie's hands and chest moving organically as part of the creature. It was maybe the closest he would ever get to seeing his wife's body move again.

Camille smelled the meat, but it was foreign to her. It was not the odor of Katie, but it would do for now. Camille instinctively trusted Roger.

"I brought you something, Camille," he said, taking some skin and muscle from the bag.

Food...

He put it on the ground between them and she crept up, biting at it with sharp, humanlike teeth. Everything about Camille was an oddity. She looked like a dozen different people blended together. Almost like a Picasso painting, but more refined. In a strange way, there was something beautiful about her.

He slowly reached his hand out to touch what was left of her hair, and she looked up at his hand, sniffing it and licking his fingers. It reminded Roger of a dog greeting someone. It was not aggressive or even the same method he had seen her devour meat with. He smiled and took out the rest of the parts, putting them near where Camille fed.

"Thank... ou..." Camille grunted.

Roger smiled. *Feel better.*

He continued to watch her eat, and shortly after, the rejuvenated, lively parts took their places on her body. She also seemed to get more attentive and clearer in her speech with each bite. She stood up on her hind legs again, her knees reverting into a more humanoid position.

She becomes more human-like, the more she feeds. Maybe this will work.

Roger scoffed at his continued thoughts of recreating Katie using this poor creature's body as the vessel. But what other choice did he have? He wanted to have one last vision of Katie before she was gone forever.

He teared up, thinking of Katie again, and stood face-to-face with Camille. He looked her up and down, admiring the patchwork appearance of her body. He put his hand up again and touched Camille's hand, which was, in actuality, a reincarnation of Katie's.

The hole in his heart felt patched. The emptiness was momentarily gone. For the first time since Katie passed, he didn't miss her—he was actually touching her again.

As Camille breathed in at his touch, the skin over the area reacted, and Camille grunted out, "Roger."

He pulled his hand back and wiped his tears, backing away. *This isn't Katie! Stop, stop, STOP!*

"I'm sorry. I have to go," Roger said, running off toward his car, leaving Camille where she stood.

He raced home and ran into his house. His mind spiraled out of control.

She can be Katie.
No, she can't. She's dead.
This is your last chance.
Make a decision and get something accomplished for once.
You are such an indecisive asshole.
No, I'm not! Just shut up. Shut your big fucking mouth!

The thoughts overwhelmed him, and he screamed at the top of his lungs. The windows in the house shook, but he didn't care if anyone heard. He kept screaming, despite his throat becoming raw and hoarse.

He then stopped and listened to his home. What was no longer *their* home. It was now just *his* home. Nothing was touched or moved or needed to be cleaned.

He pulled out his cell phone and saw there were no missed calls or work-related messages.

There was nothing right now. It was the first time since the funeral that he was alone with his thoughts. No Katie, no running around riding that desired wave of anxiety that he had been feeling for the last few weeks. It was just Roger by himself.

He dropped to the ground and started punching the hardwood floors in frustration. He grunted through the pain and kept hitting until the wood was fractured. A few large splinters penetrated his hand, causing blood to pool on the wood. But he kept going. Over and over again.

I have nothing. I have nothing to live for! Just some monster that I feed body parts to. What the fuck has happened to me!

He muffled another scream and stopped himself. He looked at his hands and realized how swollen they were.

"Fuck!" He looked at the nearby couch, remembering the times he and Katie napped there, snuggling with each other. He lunged at the couch, flipping it several times in the air. It landed a few feet away, upside down.

He looked at the matching green armchair and thought of Katie sleeping on it, looking extremely ill during her battle with cancer. He side-kicked it, knocking it over.

He ran toward the basement, falling on his backside and sliding most of the way down the stairs, bruising his hips and lower back. He stood up in a rage and punched at the cement wall in front of him.

"Why did you take her from me!" he yelled at anyone willing to hear him. "We were supposed to be together forever!" He then remembered Donald O'Sullivan's line from the first funeral he had crashed. *"I always thought I'd be the first one gone. That woman needed more time on this earth."*

He stopped punching the wall and was pretty sure he had cracked several bones in his hand. Totally exhausted from his rageful fit, he went into the storage area. He saw the empty space Katie had lain in. All that was left was her favorite acrylic blanket, stained and damp from her various fluids that seeped out onto it.

He fell to the ground and crawled to it, wrapping himself in it. The smell of death and decay didn't matter anymore. Roger just needed to be near Katie again. Any way he could. He sat there for a while before falling asleep in the blanket.

Chapter 18

Whiskey worked on Katie's body late into the evening. He pushed off many other projects to get this done for Roger and luckily didn't have anything urgent for Herbert. He'd never met anyone as desperate as Roger, but the man was coming from a good place. He was a young guy, not married for very long, and had lost his wife to a nasty illness. And it wasn't sudden either. She suffered, and he was forced to watch it.

Whiskey observed her naked body and envied Roger having an adoring wife who was so pretty. "You didn't need to be cremated to have a smokin' body, honey," he said to humor himself. "But you're lucky I got time for you. It's been really *dead* around here."

He poured himself his token glass of whiskey and took a sip.

"You don't really know a person until you embalm them," he said softly, taking a scraping instrument and removing some of the rotted tissue that was too decayed for him to work with. As he cleaned up her hands and feet, he looked at the damage done by Roger's creature. While some of the underlying tissue was torn up, it seemed like the monster was mostly interested in the skin.

"Well, that's interesting," he said, continuing to examine the wounds, tapping into his vast knowledge of cryptids and the supernatural. "I think I know what kind of creature your husband has been cheating on you with now." He thought back to the new book in his collection. "I think Roger found himself a ghoul."

He used his tools to sever a few other comparable bodies and sew the pieces onto Katie. He then blended the skin tone with a combination of wax and specialized cosmetics. He took a tin of potpourri and shoved it under her body, trying to shield some of the smell.

He continued talking to Katie. "I tend to use kitty litter when the odor is this bad, but for special cases, I get fancy."

He then began working on her face, which looked gaunt but not totally out of place. He shifted her eyelids and lips back into place using more wax. He carefully placed some fake eyelashes and applied light makeup, only enough to accentuate her already proven beauty.

"I think Roger is going to be really taken aback with how good you're going to look," he said.

He suddenly heard a noise near the lift and dropped his instruments. He quietly opened the door, but there was nothing inside.

"Goddamned mice. Guess Herbie has to put the traps out again." He closed the door, but the sounds continued, coming from the outside.

He traveled upstairs and out the back door to investigate, holding one of his knives. The noises turned into grunts.

Whiskey traveled to the rear of the building and saw something large sniffing and pawing at the lift leading to his office. "They call me Mr. Whiskey, but the bar's closed," he called out to the dark figure. She turned and looked at him, groaning. He looked at the parts of her that he could match to Katie's corpse, along with the other areas taken from prior bodies.

"Oh, jeez. You are busted goods, lady," he blurted out, chuckling.

The creature responded with an ear-piercing screech.

From what Roger had shared, it wasn't violent, despite loving human flesh. Whiskey stopped the humor and put his hands up. "I didn't mean anything by that. But Roger was right. You are something special."

Camille heard those words, and it made her feel less like a hideous beast. Even with her thoughts almost totally lost within this creature she had become, her subconscious was still inside somewhere.

Hate . . . Need Katie . . .

"Ro . . . ger," she said in a very raspy, hard-to-understand voice.

Whiskey was shocked to hear her speak. "No, Roger left a while ago. It's just me here."

"Kay . . . tee."

Whiskey realized she had developed a taste for Katie and wanted to keep feeding off her. She now also had some sort of bond with Roger, which further complicated the situation. He noticed she was sniffing the lift again.

"You can smell her, can't you?" he asked.

She moaned and walked over to him. She smelled his clothes because Katie's odor was on him. He quickly rubbed his soiled gloves, which still had some of the potpourri on them, all over his clothes to throw off the scent. She walked back to the lift.

Whiskey slowly backed away, not alerting the creature, and quickly ran inside, locking the doors and windows. He stuck his entire container of potpourri in the lift, hoping it threw off the smell. Within minutes, the noises stopped.

"What have I gotten myself into?" he asked, taking another drink.

Chapter 19

Roger laid in bed spooning Katie. It was a quiet Sunday morning, and they both had had a restful night. He pulled her closer and their bodies connected, feeling warmth and adoration for one another.

"I don't wanna move," Roger mumbled to her.

"I know. Me either. But we're going to have to wake up eventually. We can't stay like this forever," she responded, yawning.

Roger jumped awake the next day, shaken from the dream, still wet from the blanket he slept in. He didn't care if most of the fluids were from Katie being embalmed. They were still part of her, and that was all that mattered.

He was somewhat rested, but his awareness was blunted. He didn't feel much of anything. His hands were heavily bruised and still very swollen, and his body ached with several sore areas after his outburst. But aside from briefly recognizing it all, he felt like he was in suspended animation.

He stood up and slowly walked through the house, looking at the damage he'd caused the night before. Normally, he would be scrubbing the house clean, but he didn't care. He was exhausted. And he was dying from the inside out. He'd probably never smile again.

What's the point?

His cell and home phones both had a dozen unanswered messages and calls from overnight, some from work and others from family and Katie's friends. It didn't matter. He didn't care. It was too much effort to respond to everyone, just to make them feel validated that they were checking in on him like a charity case.

Roger walked upstairs and looked at the bedroom with a crib in it. He and Katie had planned to make that a nursery before she got sick. He hadn't touched the room in almost two years. It was too painful for him to think about. The minute he cleaned the room or got rid of the furniture, his hopes of having children with Katie would be gone forever. And that, much like her death, was something else that he wasn't properly able to process.

The crib was the first piece of the nursery they had inherited from a family member upon announcing they were trying to get pregnant. But they lost three pregnancies that they were aware of. Katie was stronger than him. She braved through, never afraid to keep trying, while Roger was always hesitant. His self-awareness at the time wasn't as keen as it was present day. He always thought he was trying to save his wife from the heartbreak of another loss, but it wasn't for her. It had always been for him.

Roger changed clothes and drove over to His and Hearse Funeral Home in the late morning. He didn't eat beforehand and had no appetite or feelings to do anything other than see his wife again. To see just how good Mr. Whiskey was at his job. Roger walked down the small staircase, ignoring the hilarious signs Whiskey had hung all over the walls, and knocked.

"Come on in, Roger," Whiskey yelled.

Whiskey stood in front of his wall of freezer containers for the bodies. Roger hadn't seen the work area and his office so neat and put together. It came across very professional, except for Whiskey's Jim Beam belt buckle holding up his worn blue jeans, and today's shirt that read *What's the worst part of having sex? Getting caught by the mortician.*

* * *

Whiskey held his hands behind his back humbly with his shoulders squared. He took note of Roger's bruised hands and altered gait.

"Rough night?" he asked. "Not a *mourning* person?" He waited for a chuckle from Roger. "Spelled m-o-u, not m-o-r . . . never mind."

Whiskey paused and evaluated the truly distraught state of his friend. He needed to say something to bring Roger back from the brink of insanity. Whiskey didn't have any friends and was never good at making them. But he'd connected with Roger in a unique way, even among these strange circumstances. And Whiskey didn't like the thought of losing his only friend when he could have at least tried to help him.

"So, Roger, I've been doing this for a fairly long time now..."

Roger prepared himself, expecting bad news about Katie's body.

"I've had some tough cases in my twenty years, but Katie was up there. However, I think you'll be pleased with how she came out."

Roger breathed deeply as Whiskey put his hand on the handle of the freezer area with Katie's body inside.

"Are you ready?"

Roger nodded, lowering his head.

Whiskey gently pulled the body out and hoped Roger was pleased with what he had done.

Roger raised his head and saw his wife, almost as if she had just died a moment before. Her milky white skin was back to its pristine state. There were no more IV marks, scars, blemishes, or any imperfections. She wore a blue headband, blue lipstick, light mascara, and a matching shirt that showed part of her collarbone area and décolletage. Roger could tell Whiskey chose that color to make some of the skin discoloration seem less obvious in certain areas.

Her blonde hair looked fuller and was brushed off to the side, just as it had been at her funeral. The sagging of her lips and eyes had been fixed completely, and her angelic face and small, slightly pointed nose were on point. And the smell was almost totally gone, masked with some type of potpourri.

Roger's chest constricted and his eyes filled with tears. He hoped she would open those gorgeous blue eyes and tell him she loved him one last time.

"I love you, Roger," he heard Katie say in his mind.

* * *

Whiskey stood in silence, no longer making his tasteless jokes or morbid puns. Roger seemed to appreciate what Whiskey had done. He started to speak, but Roger grabbed him hard and hugged him. Whiskey was caught off guard and didn't return the embrace for several seconds while he collected his thoughts.

"Thank you," Roger said with his face buried in Whiskey's shirt. "Thank you, my friend."

Whiskey was honored that Roger was not only happy with his hard work but now considered him a friend too. He wasn't being silly when he had previously told Roger about the life of a mortician. It *was* lonely. He was always on call, never took vacations, worked with dead bodies, and had a really bizarre personality that was not appealing to most people. So finding friends and significant others was very hard for him. But he had enjoyed his time with Roger, and now it was clear the feeling was mutual.

They stepped apart, both looking at Katie.

"God, she looks so good. Like all she has to do is open those eyes and everything will be okay," Roger said, wiping his eyes.

"She was a really beautiful woman, Roger. Not sure what she was doing with you, amigo." Whiskey broke up the somber tone, adjusting his constantly slanted glasses.

* * *

Roger let out a forced laugh and put his hand on Katie's arm. It looked better than it felt, and reality set in that this was extremely temporary. Despite Whiskey's best efforts, he had forewarned Roger that even his best work would not last long at all. He remembered how Katie's skin felt on Camille. It was alive, and it felt real because it was.

Whiskey took off his glasses and held them in front of his waist with both hands. "Hey, Rog . . . I'm really happy you like how she came out," he started. "And I hate to kill the mood here. But, uh, if she lasts like this until tomorrow, I'd be really surprised. I had to do a ton of extensive work just to make this happen. I was able to retain most of her body but had to supplement with other people's parts and a ton of cosmetics. I was really just hoping to let you say goodbye on your own terms with your wife. Her funeral, that hospital room she was stuck in when it happened . . . none of that should've happened. But here, you can say your goodbyes and we can proceed with the cremation. It's the only way to do this right."

Exhausted, Roger looked at Whiskey and nodded, knowing it was the hard truth. "I know." He again thought of Camille wearing Katie's skin.

You can still do this on your own terms, Roger. Don't you want to see her eyes one last time?

"Hey, Rog, I'll give you some time with her alone, if you'd like. To say your goodbyes and all. But we really should talk about the monster some more. She was here last night."

Roger finally took his eyes off his wife and looked at Whiskey again. "She was here?" he asked, confused.

"Yeah, it was sniffing around. No pun intended. I think she was here for Katie."

"Why do you say that?"

"Well, why else would she be here like that? You said she was at your house with the body and then suddenly found her way here once you brought Katie. She's got a scent and taste for her now, Roger. I think ghouls establish some sort of connection with the first body they consume as a ghoul."

Roger wasn't sure what to say.

"So, again, once you say goodbye, we have to get this body burned so it stops following you and me around like that. We don't know what kind of stuff we're dealing with there."

Frustration filled Roger. He was going to lose both Camille and Katie in one swift action.

"She's not an *it*. Her name is Camille. And I thought you were some expert on this nerdy shit," Roger snapped at his friend.

Whiskey stepped back, raising his hands, taken aback by the verbal assault. "Hey, hey, easy, tiger. This is a *dead* end. Final nail in the coffin. However you wanna say it. It's gotta stop here before someone gets hurt." He hesitated before continuing. "And I know what Camille is too."

Roger settled himself and breathed deeper to control his anxiety. "What is she then, Einstein?" Roger shot out.

Whiskey blinked and shook his head at the obvious insult but didn't lose his signature calm, cool demeanor. "Like I already said, I think she's a ghoul."

"A ghoul?"

"Yes. I'm not certain, but between what I saw myself and all the things you described, if I'm mistaken, I'm not far off either."

Roger breathed again and tried to keep an open mind on the matter. "Okay, so what can you tell me about ghouls?"

"Okay, hang with me here. I'm gonna freestyle all this, so try to stay with me."

Roger took a step back and leaned on a metal table.

"You say she keeps going back to that cemetery. That's a calling card of a ghoul. And you told me she claimed to be from Meadowsville. We all know the story there. Weird stuff happened. Vampires, gods and devils, and whatever else. It's not far-fetched to imagine that she was turned into something when the disaster happened."

"So how do you become a ghoul?"

"From what I've seen and read over the years, you have to eat human flesh."

"That's it?"

Whiskey chuckled at the comment. "Well, it's not that simple, Roger. You eat flesh and you're kinda reborn into a ghoul. I think it's called *divine punishment* or whatever religious term. You eat flesh, and you need to continue eating it to survive. If you don't, you kind of wither and die. And the longer you're like that, the harder it is to have even an ounce of humanity inside. You basically are destined to lose to the creature and eventually revert back into the true form of a ghoul."

Roger remembered Camille's speech improving each time she ate and how her body kept transforming based on her intake.

"Well, what about the graveyard thing? What significance does that have?" Roger asked.

"Honestly, I haven't had a chance to check further into my library of monsters and unknown creatures. So I'm not sure. I just know that they tend to stay around cemeteries."

Roger saw the obvious, direct links but was keen on another, more believable explanation. "Okay, I can see some of that, but why is she hunting Katie and not hurting me?"

Whiskey smiled smugly. "Because she already had a taste of Katie at some point, and she knew you'd continue bringing her food. Ghouls pick certain types of people and prey on them."

"So—what? You're calling me weak and vulnerable?" Roger snapped again.

"Whoa, whoa. Take it down a notch. Grab a cold one and relax, big guy." Whiskey put a hand on Katie's table, wincing at the expression.

Roger wasn't amused by yet another joke, especially at his wife's expense. "Stop with the fucking jokes. I mean it." He balled his fists.

Whiskey scolded himself for such an ill-timed remark. "Okay, I'm sorry. That was stupid. I'm nervous. But I just care for your safety here. I'm not trying to make you angry. I'm just giving you the facts," he stammered.

Roger put a hand on Katie, looking down at her again, using her to calm his thoughts.

"And Roger, I'm not going to be able to give you any more parts after this."

"If it's a money thing, I'll pay—"

Whiskey put up his hand. "It's not a money thing. It's a moral dilemma. I shouldn't be taking from other people to help myself. And especially not for money. It's not right." He walked to his desk and handed Roger all of the cash he'd been given.

Angry at the boundary now being set, Roger tossed the piles of cash down on the floor.

"I may have done some stupid things in this job, but if someone ever caught me, I'd be done. I have nothing else but this job. No friends, no girlfriend, no family, really, and the reason I go out of my way in this job is because I know I can't help myself. So I take pride in helping others."

Roger was still angry but truly listened to what Whiskey was sharing with him.

"But that's my journey. A dead body and a glass of whiskey. That's it and that's fine. I provide a service and get paid for it. But most of all, Roger, I can't do anything to hurt you."

Befuddled, Roger asked, "Hurt me by helping me?"

"No, by enabling you. This whole adventure you've been on. It's a distraction. Your wife died. And that's an awful thing that no one should ever have to experience, but it happened and that's reality. Playing with unknown monsters in graveyards, sewing people together to keep Katie's lifeless body here just for yourself . . . none of this is kosher."

Roger's irritation grew again. "So you're telling me that you're done with all this? Done with me?" He kicked the cash, scattering it all over the preparation room.

Whiskey looked around at the raining bills and sighed. "Roger, you know how people are trained to deal with addicts and those who are not only endangering themselves but others too?"

Roger slammed a door in the freezer area, hurting his already sore hands. He knew the answer from the health counseling and leadership training portions of his education.

"You set the boundaries, and if they still push you to continue the unhealthy and damaging situation, you have to cut them off. It's for their own good—and to protect you too. But the hope is that it's enough of a jolt to wake them up and get back on a better track. If not, you're at least saving yourself from a bad situation and no longer helping them hurt themselves."

* * *

Whiskey felt terrible issuing this ultimatum, but he knew it was for Roger's own good. He was clearly not taking care of himself and not dealing with Katie's passing. He'd be dead in the not-too-distant future if he didn't stop what he was doing.

Roger paced for a moment then turned back to Whiskey. "I want Katie's body on that lift tonight. I'll be stopping by to get her. And you'd better not stop me."

Whiskey was concerned and felt threatened.

"What are you going to do here, Roger? I'm really worried about you. I don't want you getting hurt. And I don't want you doing anything that you'll regret."

Roger shot Whiskey a look of pure rage. "Worried about me enough to cut me off because I'm some head case. Thanks a lot, Whiskey. Have fun being alone with your bodies making jokes about deadlifts, suicides, and whatever other weird shit you have in that fucked-up head of yours. No wonder you're alone. You act like you're better than someone like me. But you're not. You're just as fucked up as I am. You're just too afraid to admit it to yourself."

That comment cut through Whiskey like a fresh scalpel. Fighting with Roger would only make this situation worse. He needed to do what was best to rid himself of all this and hope Roger made the right decisions.

"Roger, I'm sorry if anything I said hurt you. I don't want to fight, and I think of you as a friend, whether you want to believe that or not. I'll have Katie in the lift by nine tonight, well past when Herbie upstairs has left for the evening."

Roger nodded, collected himself, and left, fuming at Whiskey. But he was also angry that he'd let himself get this far gone and was now isolating himself from everyone. He was losing it all, and he was the one allowing it to happen. It would all be different if he could just see Katie one more time so he could move on.

I have no choice . . .

Chapter 20

That night, Roger returned to the funeral home. He spent the rest of that day lying in Katie's blanket in the storage room again. He lay there in a comatose state until it got dark outside. His body screamed for food, but he ignored it all.

This is what Camille must feel like when she's hungry.

He pulled his sedan to the back area by the body lift and opened it to see Katie. Her body was already starting to fall apart again. Whiskey was right about that. Roger then noticed a note on the lift that read "Roger, I'm sorry we got so heated earlier. My door is always open. Best wishes. MW."

Gee, thanks, Whiskey. You piss in my face and hang me out to dry.

He tried to move the body but couldn't. Between his battered hands, dehydration and starvation, lack of sleep, and everything else working against him, he had very little strength. Definitely not enough to pick up a several-hundred-pound body by himself.

He attempted to do it anyway and ended up falling down. He tried several more times but couldn't budge the body, and everything started to fall apart in his hands. He sat on the cold pavement, sweaty, frustrated, and tired. He looked down to see Camille hunched over, sniffing at his hands as she detected Katie.

She looked away from Roger and toward the body.

This is your last and only chance to make this happen. "Camille, you can have her now." His stomach turned upside down as soon as he said it.

Katie, they both thought simultaneously.

Camille grunted and brazenly began clawing at Katie's body, tearing off the clothes that Whiskey so delicately placed on her. Roger watched the magic happen as Camille placed her extended tongue on Katie's calves. He remembered rubbing her legs at night sometimes, especially when she was sick. The chemotherapy treatments gave her the worst swelling in that area, so his efforts were always appreciated.

The skin began to detach from the wax and cosmetics that Whiskey used, pulling it off the stiffened, rotting musculature. Camille then clamped her large teeth around the eroding bones of the legs, crushing them like candy.

As she continued to dine on Katie, Roger watched Camille's rather immediate transformation. As each part was ingested, it became a part of Camille.

Katie's legs appeared, then her waist, then her stomach and arms, and Roger felt like this was the most beautiful, fulfilling moment of his life.

Katie's sculpted shoulder blades evolved into her kissable neck. Then the brown hair transitioned to blonde on Camille's head, like a chameleon taking on the color of its surroundings. Camille turned to Roger, with the last thing to eat being Katie's face. Everything looked like his wife except the hideous face that Camille now called her own.

She turned back to Katie and finished the face.

There's my girl. There's my Katie.

Aside from some small puddles of fluid left on the asphalt, Katie's body was gone. Camille now stood there, looking almost identical to Katie in all her glory. She looked human, but any aspect of Camille withered away quickly. Despite the ingestion of Katie's body, something was different. Camille didn't regain any part of herself. She barely had any intuition left. She had now fully evolved into this monstrous ghoul. And Roger was not a friend. He was her prey.

"Oh my God," Roger eked out, looking at the reincarnation of his wife. "It's really you."

Katie stood before him, almost like he remembered her. She didn't look sick anymore. Like her cancer never happened. This was Katie at her best. Roger started to cry, thankful for this opportunity. Suddenly, Camille was an afterthought and Katie took full precedence.

He stood up as they stared at each one another.

"I have clothes. Let me get you something to cover up." He turned to the car.

"No, Roger." Katie gently placed her hand on his arm.

His heart skipped a beat, and he turned to her again.

"Just hold me, Roger," she said, hugging him.

Roger cried harder than he had since Katie's funeral. "I never thought I'd see you again. I've missed you so much," he said, holding her tight.

He looked down and noticed a few small areas of her body didn't exactly match the rest of her but ignored it. She grabbed his face and they kissed. Roger felt her lips, teeth, and tongue. This was Katie. Even if it was the last time he'd see her and hold her. He would be content with it. The most important thing was that they were here together. And he just needed to enjoy the moment.

I love her so much.

"Roger, I need you to do something for me, sweetie." She guided his face to look at her, locking him into her blue eyes.

Oh God, those eyes. Those perfect baby blues looking at me.

"Do you want me to stay here with you?" she asked.

Roger nodded his head, entranced by his wife.

"Sweetie, I need meat."

Roger got angry again at Whiskey.

"I can't get you anymore, honey. I don't know what to do."

Katie looked at him, feigning the supposed discord happening in her new body. "I need live meat." She almost hissed out like a snake, caressing the side of his face. "Live meat lets me stay like this for longer. Would you like that?"

Under her spell, Roger uttered, "Yes. Yes, I do. I want you here with me."

You could feed her Whiskey. Whiskey deserves it.

"No," he mumbled to himself, knowing he would never do that to his friend.

"Roger, I need you. If I don't get meat, I'll wither away and die. Just like before. You don't want that to happen, do you?"

"No," he said sternly and determined. "I'll figure it out. I'll get you fresh meat."

She took Roger's hand and put it under her nose, sniffing it, remembering his scent. He would never be able to evade her now.

"Rog . . . er . . . run . . ." The final bits of Camille fought to regain any control, but it was futile.

The ghoul was using its sexuality and Roger's weakness to its advantage.

Chapter 21

Roger sat during a funeral at the His and Hearse the next day. This had become his go-to site now, and he knew Camille would be close by. And he had never seen Mr. Whiskey leave the basement area, so there should be no concern. Roger couldn't stop anything now.

He sat in the front row at the funeral, looking at the deceased, a man in his early sixties. His cell phone vibrated, and he saw a message from Eric at Tick Tech Logistics.

> Hey, Roger. Hadn't heard from you in a bit and just wanted to check in. The procedure went well, and nothing was found. Thank you for all your help!

Look at that. You've never neglected the people that work with you. You've lost complete focus and control of yourself.

Roger took a deep breath, becoming frustrated with himself. As if it weren't bad enough his personal life was in shambles, now his professional life was suffering too. He quickly put the phone back in his pocket.

He stood up and looked at the deceased man's push-broom mustache and chiseled features. Much like Katie and every other body he'd seen after being prepared by Mr. Whiskey, he simply looked like someone who was comfortably napping. Roger didn't even know the name of this person. And he didn't care. He just looked at the parts of the body like he was at a deli counter at the grocery store.

It's all meat, just prepared differently.

He looked around at the somewhat younger group, which was perfect. Whatever Camille/Katie was fed, she would take on the features of whoever the victim was. He wanted to keep whoever was brought to her as close to Katie as possible. And there were several women who could be obtained here.

To avoid arousing suspicion, he began walking around, looking at the pictures and memorabilia of the deceased. He saw one young woman who had light brown hair, dressed very conservatively in a silky blouse and pressed dress pants. She was a little shorter than Katie, but her body shape matched up fairly well.

Roger continued to stare at her, imagining Katie devouring her little by little.

Would she start from the feet and work up? Or the head and work down? Would she keep this person alive while she dined?

He brandished a sinister smile and started to go introduce himself when a much larger man came up behind her and placed a hand firmly on her hip. Roger recognized the type of touch, which, with the absence of wedding bands, indicated he was this woman's boyfriend.

Strike one.

He walked by and entered into one of the smaller side rooms. Another lone woman sat by herself, blotting tears as she looked at her smartphone. She peered up at him with large brown eyes.

Fuck, they're not blue.

She flashed a polite smile and looked back down at her phone. Roger viewed her hand and saw she also wasn't wearing a wedding band. He sat on an ugly yellow patterned sofa directly across from her. To keep up appearances, he began thinking of Katie in the hospital and started to shed tears, knowing the woman would offer him a tissue from the box on a table to her right.

She didn't look up, so Roger sniffled a few times to get her attention. He felt her eyes on him and shifted around in his seat, pretending to check for something to address the tears.

"Here," she said in a soft voice, offering him the box of tissues.

He looked up and met her eyes, smiling.

Of all the fucking women here. Why can't her eyes match Katie's?

"Thank you," he said, walking over and taking one from her. "I may need more. Do you mind?" He motioned to the opposite end of the couch.

"Not at all. I'm Amy." She extended her hand to him after putting her phone in her purse.

Roger's animalistic urges rose as he surveyed his prey.

You're no better than that ghoul is. You know that?

I am better. I have my Katie back. That's all that mattered. Seeing her once wasn't enough. I need her for longer.

"I'm Roger," he said calmly, shaking her hand.

"How did you know Paul? Where you a friend of Xavier's? Or Henry's?"

It can't be this easy.

You're scum. Absolute scum.

"Yeah, Xavier. We're old friends. I used to be really close with the family. I heard about this and had to come pay my respects. Paul was always such a nice person," Roger said, making up the story and hoping it went over with Amy.

She nodded.

"How about you?" he asked in kind way.

"Paul used to be my boss a while back. We kept in touch. I also went to school with Henry, but I was never friends with him."

Roger stared deep into her eyes again, thinking of how easily the skin would peel away from her soft tissues. How he would eventually be kissing those lips, even after they no longer belonged to her.

Congratulations! You've hit rock bottom. And you're now being dragged along it.

Shut up!

"Death is never an easy thing. Like, one minute they're there, and the next they're gone."

She agreed and was fully attentive to him. Roger hoped no one else entered the room and interrupted him trying to manipulate this poor girl.

"This is the first time that I've lost someone. Even my grandparents are still alive. It's just all new to me."

Perfect.

"I just lost my wife not too long ago." He was too impatient to wait on bringing in the big guns to help this situation along.

"Oh, my goodness, you poor thing," she said, putting a hand to her open mouth and shocked face.

"Yeah, that was really hard. Still is. But you just have to appreciate the time you had with the person. Be thankful for that. And know that they'll always be alive in your heart," he said, genuinely starting to cry now, thinking of Katie again.

Fuck, I blew it. Bail!

Roger looked up at her as she joined him in tears. This innocent person in mourning.

It's bad enough she is distraught over a loss like this, and look at you. Big man. Gonna take this young, innocent girl and feed her to a ghoul. Just to appease whatever it is this will do for you. This is by far the worst thing you've ever considered doing. Katie would be ashamed of you for this. Not that thing outside. The real Katie.

Roger let his tears fall and got up quickly, at war with himself. He looked at Amy, who appeared sympathetic.

"It was a pleasure meeting you, Amy. If you'll excuse me, I must—" He quickly walked toward the exit.

"Roger, wait," she called out.

But he continued outside.

Roger, she can't follow you. This is a trap, and you know it. Tell her to go back inside!

"Roger," she called again, approaching him quickly as he circled toward the back of the funeral home.

"Roger. . ."

He heard the sound from the woods surrounding the small parking lot. There was a single overhead light that illuminated only three quarters of the lot, not including the farthest area. That was where he heard the voice.

Katie . . . you're here.

Like a sailor to a siren, he continued walking to the sound, no longer hearing Amy behind him.

Amy grabbed his arm. "Hey, slow down," she said.

She's done it to herself. It's her own fault.

You can still fix this. You have to get her away from Katie.

Roger, still crying and battling himself, turned to her and saw her big brown eyes were as glassy as his were.

"Roger, it's okay. I can't imagine how hard this has been for you. But we're all here for you. For each other."

Roger remembered his dad saying that same thing at Katie's funeral. And he realized in that moment he'd been avoiding the wonderful people he had in his life. Katie was gone, but everyone else was still there. And they all wanted him to be okay and were even willing to help. All those voicemails and texts he'd ignored and even the people at his worksites. They all meant well. Roger was the one isolating himself and allowing all this to work against his recovery from losing Katie.

Roger turned to the shadow-cloaked area of the lot and heard his name again. Katie's naked form appeared just beyond those shadows.

"Who's that?" Amy asked, now noticing Katie.

Roger panicked and grabbed both of her hands, now more fearful than upset.

Amy's eyes widened when saw his face, seeing something was very wrong.

Save her. Stop being selfish and save her. You cannot let her die for you.

Roger regained total clarity. He had gone too far. With Amy, with Katie, with all of it. Whiskey was right. And now Roger was acting like the complete antithesis of who he really was—a caring, supportive, and empathetic person. He quickly realized the seriousness of the situation in front of him.

"Amy . . . I need you to listen to me and not ask any questions. Please go back inside and lock those doors. I know you don't know me. But you need to trust me. And don't tell anyone what you saw here, or they'll all be in danger."

Amy looked at him, unsure.

Roger turned and saw Katie now under the light, running a hand gently over her chest. Her beautiful body had already started to fall apart. Patches of her skin were flapping around, and her face was distorted.

He turned back to Amy. "Do you understand what I just told you, Amy? You have to go now. *Now!*" he yelled.

She took off toward the funeral home, breaking one of her heels in the process.

Roger turned to face Katie, who now also sounded different. He was surprised how quickly her body had broken down since yesterday. But he recalled Whiskey saying how much synthetic material he added when he rejuvenated her. And Katie had told him live meat would make everything last longer.

"Why? Roger, we needed her," she asked, clearly distraught as she approached him.

Roger couldn't respond and was mesmerized by her mere presence.

You're stronger than this. Fight!

"Roger, you're going to let me die again. You could've saved me this time. We could be together forever." She was now face-to-face with him.

You're stronger than this.

"No, you needed her. I didn't. This isn't right. And you're not Katie."

Katie pulled Roger hard and kissed him. It lingered for several seconds, but Roger did not reciprocate the passionate embrace. Roger recognized it didn't taste like Katie because this wasn't her.

This isn't your wife. This is a ghoul who is preying on your vulnerabilities. You owe Whiskey an apology for trying to save your life. And Eric and everyone else. It's time to make this right.

Katie pulled away from him.

"You're not Katie. You're not even Camille. You're just some ugly, evil monster." Roger began to struggle.

"Roger, how can you say that. Look at me." She began moving awkwardly, and Katie's body now resembled a sheet of skin loosely hanging over something else underneath. She tried to lick his face and bite his hand, but he pushed her off.

The ghoul grunted and sized him up.

Roger knew couldn't physically fight this phantom. Especially not in his current state. *This might be it for me.*

"Whoa, whoa, folks. Hang on a minute," a voice said from behind.

Whiskey?

Both he and the ghoul saw Whiskey jogging with a covered metal cart, looking as average as only he could be. Roger saw his shirt that read *Throat Lozenges Prevent Coffin*.

Roger smiled and was so thankful for a friend like Mr. Whiskey right now. Whiskey stopped the cart and straightened himself out, like a comedian about to go on stage.

"I heard all the noise out here and thought I could help." Whiskey pulled the sheet off the cart, displaying a full upper torso of a woman. "Now, I know how difficult Roger can be. Believe me. But this should at least tide you over until we can get you some fresh meat, Camille. Or Katie. Or do you prefer another name?"

The ghoul purred at both men, looking back and forth between them. It then shoved Roger to the side, unhinging its jaws and devouring the torso like a competitive eater. Its now enlarged teeth snapped and gnashed together as it watched a weary Whiskey back up.

Whiskey, I hope you know what you're doing here.

The ghoul stopped chewing and began to gag. It vomited up pieces of the torso, splattering the organs on the ground, which splashed on both men. Several pieces of skin fell off the ghoul as its body began to enlarge. It twitched as it shed most of Katie's skin, some of which now hung like strands of cloth off of its large, boney, and exposed muscular frame. The hands and feet grew, claws emerging from extremely long arms.

Whiskey grabbed Roger and pulled him away.

The ghoul pounded the asphalt, damaging the lot. Its back separated, with a line of sharp vertebrae jutting out. Its true face erupted, tossing Katie's skin all around. The large maw was surrounded by jagged teeth. But Katie's blue eyes remained.

She's still in there somewhere.

The creature vomited more and stumbled, the torso clearly not agreeing with it. The ghoul lunged toward both men but winced in pain and fell back several times. It was injured and dying. All its previous meals had been ejected from its body. Its strength was nearly gone, and its livelihood was in serious peril unless it fed again and quickly. But with Roger and Whiskey no longer an option, the future was bleak and death was imminent. It screeched and retreated in a sloppily executed run back to the cemetery.

The last part of Camille inside it rejoiced, knowing Roger and Whiskey had outsmarted the beast.

* * *

Roger looked at Whiskey, who hugged him.

"Almost lost ya there, buddy."

Roger hugged him right back. "I'm sorry, Whiskey. I was an idiot. You were right. About all of it," he said.

"No need for any of that now. You're okay. That's the main thing." Whiskey patted Roger's head softly, grabbing some of his hair.

"What did you do to it?"

Whiskey dusted his shoulders off and wiped off his signature belt buckle. "Whoever told you being a fan of monsters and cryptids was a waste? It teaches you some useful information. Like that fact that ghouls can't digest real food. It hurts them very badly. So when you feed one a torso stuffed with all the goodies from my mini fridge downstairs, well . . . not a good mix."

Roger shook his head in amazement. "I have to make sure this is finished tonight. I can't let this happen to anyone else." He looked toward the path to the cemetery.

"I know. Finish this thing and get back here for a drink. Go say goodbye to your Katie."

This is it. This is really it. She'll really be gone forever after this. Every single part of her. Go make your peace.

Roger stood up and began walking to his car. "No jokes this time?"

Whiskey smirked. "I had one about a girl telling me 'over her dead body' once. And then she ended up on my table. Something along those lines. It wasn't ready yet. Sorry."

Roger turned, upset but still somehow smiling, hoping to one day hear the joke when Whiskey had perfected it.

"Oh, and Roger, you don't have to call me Whiskey anymore. Name's Larry. Larry Lumpkin."

Roger smiled. "And I thought my name was bad . . . Larry." He laughed, trying not to cry and finally feeling clearheaded. "Roger Todger and Larry Lumpkin. What a pair we make."

Larry smiled back, watching his friend leave, knowing he would finally be okay.

Chapter 22

Roger entered the cemetery, clearly hearing the dying ghoul atop the crypt. It sounded like a lion breathing heavily. But the breaths weren't evenly spaced, and they sounded very labored. An occasional grunt emerged too.

He climbed the crypt and saw the ghoul laid out. Every breath made its large body rise and fall. It was no longer dangerous. It just looked at him with Katie's eyes—the last remaining part of her as he sat down.

"Katie, I know this isn't you. But I need to make peace with everything that's happened." He extended his legs, and his body relaxed. He looked up at the clear sky, and more tears came down his dirtied face. "I'm so angry you were taken from me. I'm so frustrated we didn't have more time together. And have babies. And get angry at the news together.

And bicker about what movies to watch. And grow old, laughing at each other as we fell apart. All of that. We should have had all of it."

The monster continued to watch him as he poured his heart out. Camille recognized Roger but had no sense of awareness at this point. She was tired of fighting. She had lost this battle and needed to be at peace with her transition.

"We only had a little bit of time. And I know we should be thankful we even had that. Some people never find their great loves. But we did. We were very lucky. We both were." He patted the ghoul's gnarled, hideous foot. "I've made a lot of mistakes. Hurt a lot of people. Been very ignorant and stupid." He began to cry again. "And I'm so sorry that I wasn't able to let you go when you died." He took a deep breath. "You leaving me . . . tore my heart in half. The last few years watching you suffer. I always thought the doctors would tell us you'd get through it and be just fine. All that hard work would pay off." He rubbed his forehead, smudging some dirt. "But things didn't work out like that. I know that you're not in pain anymore. But it hurts me so bad to have to continue to live without you." Tears trickled down his face.

"This is supposed to be a hard thing to process. It's not easy or simple, and all of this stuff I'm feeling is okay." He leaned forward. "But it has to come to an end now. As much as I wish there was some other way." He gently bit his lower lip, preparing for his final words to her. "I'll never forget you. I always have and always will love you." He slowly removed his hand from the ghoul's body.

Camille evolved into something beyond physical form. She was at peace, just as Katie and Roger were.

The ghoul's blue eyes closed for the last time, and its body disintegrated within seconds. And all traces of Katie were gone.

Roger sat on top of the crypt until the morning, watching the sky change colors and thinking of the good times with his wife. He had to make some big changes in his life. Katie would want him to continue living. He needed to reconnect with his family and their friends and develop new relationships with the people he'd been lucky to encounter on this journey. And he needed to refocus on work and continue helping all the people who depended on him. He needed to become himself again. Not just himself, but a new and improved version of himself. On a new trajectory in his life. He smiled at the thought.

That sounds nice.

* * *

In the early morning, after the sun rose, he climbed down and left the cemetery.

Father Clark walked his poodle again near the entrance. He saw Roger and turned away, not wanting another unpleasant confrontation.

Roger, with a new lease on life, approached him anyway. "Listen, Father Clark..."

The priest turned back toward Roger with a very stern face.

"I . . . um . . . just want to apologize. I was out of line the other day. I know you were just trying to be helpful."

Father Clark was shocked by Roger's change of heart.

"Maybe when I'm ready one day, I'll come visit you here. But thank you for being so nice." He extended his hand.

Father Clark smiled and shook it.

Roger then returned home with a renewed sense of purpose.

Chapter 23

Several weeks passed, and Roger returned to his house after another long day at work. But it was a good feeling—a sense of satisfaction from a hard day's effort. He once again took pride in his daily performance. And with his new routine, where he practiced a more sensible and consistent self-care regimen, he felt completely focused and rejuvenated.

Home sweet home.

He checked his watch and realized he had only an hour to spare before meeting Larry Lumpkin for a drink. "God, that name. It may be worse than mine..." He chuckled.

They agreed to start going out to bars instead of meeting exclusively at the funeral home, with the ambition of being more social together. Which would take some of the pressure off of them being among the *living* individually.

Just leave the goofy shirts home, Roger told Larry through text. Wear something that doesn't make you seem as weird as I know you really are.

Roger, you're so humerus, Larry responded sarcastically.

Roger went inside and saw he had two new voicemails. He listened to the first, an obvious spam call concerning the IRS. The second was from his father-in-law, Franklin, just to check in.

It had taken Roger several days after the events concluded with the ghoul to return each message and thank everyone for their concern, apologizing for his absence. They all appreciated the callbacks and continued to be present for him, for which he was thankful. He also got in touch with Donald O'Sullivan and invited him out with for a beer with Larry and him, like they had talked about at Carrie's funeral.

Donald opened up the conversation by calling Roger a son of a bitch but not in a nasty way. He was surprised but very happy to hear from Roger. With the three of them out drinking, who knew what kind of shenanigans they would be up to. And it would hopefully be the first of many such occasions.

He walked upstairs to shower, noticing several open areas of the house. He had begun donating some of Katie's possessions, which had been hard to relinquish, but he was looking ahead to brighter days. Holding on to the past would have been painful and damaging, and he was ready to progress past that.

As he reached the bathroom, his cell phone rang. The name on the screen was Allison Miller.

He couldn't believe that even with his lazy responses to her after the O'Sullivan funeral, she was still trying to get ahold of him. He wasn't sure he was ready for any type of relationship yet, but he had to try. He didn't need to rush anything, and he was hopeful she would understand his situation and his stage of the grieving process. He couldn't control everything but had to at least be open to new experiences now.

This is okay. You got this.

He also wondered whether Katie would approve of him even thinking about being friendly with another woman. But he reminded himself that even if he began dating someone like Allison, it wouldn't be to replace Katie. Katie would always be there in his memories and in his heart. And he would learn to love again, in whatever form or person it came in. Or learn to live alone.

He was ready for anything.

"Hi, Allison." He answered the phone ready to truly begin his new life.

www.ingramcontent.com/pod-product-compliance
Lightning Source LLC
LaVergne TN
LVHW041840070526
838199LV00045BA/1362